KISS ME NOW

MELANIE JACOBSON

CHAPTER ONE

Ian

I slipped on my sunglasses and tugged my baseball cap lower as I watched the wife of the third most powerful man in American politics slip out of the cheap apartment she'd rented for trysts with her pool boy. I didn't bother sliding lower in the driver's seat. It would only draw her attention. That was the last thing I wanted.

Washington DC and the people who ran it never failed to be a cliché. I snapped a few pictures with a telephoto lens. She walked down the street to the Mercedes she always parked two blocks away. As if she were fooling anyone.

Well, she was fooling her husband. He had no idea. It was midafternoon. My subject had to spend her evenings on her husband's arm at his various soirees and receptions, so Pool Boy got the daylight hours. I wondered what she told her husband she did with her days. The spa? Charity luncheons?

I settled in to wait for her boyfriend. An hour had passed with no action when my dash display lit up with an incoming call from my favorite person on earth. For the first time all day, I smiled and answered.

"Hey, Gran."

"Hi, honey. I'm not disrupting your work, am I?"

"No, it's fine. What's up?"

"Ian Greene, you better not work too late." Gran's voice held her usual note of concern.

"Gran, you know most people work until dinner time, right? It's the middle of the afternoon. I'm not in danger of overworking myself." It wasn't exactly a lie. I might work long hours most days, but today I could tell her with a clear conscience that as of the time of this phone call, I had not yet overworked.

"I know you work way past suppertime most days, Ian. You need to take better care of yourself."

The apartment door opened as she spoke, and I scooped up my camera and trained it on the young guy emerging.

"I'm fine, Gran. I promise." *Click, click.* "Now tell me about you. How's life on the mean streets of Creekville?" I made sure I had the apartment number in the shot. *Click.*

Gran laughed. "Well, Gertie Meyer got her hair colored a red that doesn't naturally grow on any human head, and then she got her eyebrows tattooed on, and Lois told her at canasta the other morning that she ought to sign up to appear as a clown at the church fair, and now they aren't speaking."

I smiled, amused at the scandals that rocked Gran's town. It was refreshing after the truly heinous ones I regularly uncovered in DC. I snapped a couple more pictures, making sure to capture Pool Boy's fit physique. That was really going to bug the husband. "I can't believe Lois said that to her. That sounds downright mean, even for her."

"I'd agree except that when Gertie swanned in with her ridiculous new hair color, she told Lois that her sweater made her look like she was smuggling two different sized melons in her bra, so Gertie had it coming."

I laughed. "Good for Lois, then. I'd love to have seen that argument." Pool Boy rounded the corner, and I set the camera on the passenger seat. Once again, all the players involved had behaved in predictably corrupt ways, and I had the evidence we needed for our client. It was unfortunate that I could reliably expect the nation's elite to be on their worst possible behavior, but hey, it paid the bills. Handsomely.

"You can see Gertie and Lois spar anytime you want to, you know," Gran said. "I keep telling you to come and see me. I worry about you, breathing in all that dirty air."

"You usually accuse the capital of hot air."

"Only the politicians are full of hot air. And not all of them. Lots of truly good-hearted people do their best there. You just happen to spend all your time working with the bad ones."

"Not *with* them. More like working *on* them, taking them down."

"It's jaded you. You forget they're the tiny fraction. But in this case, I meant the actual pollution, anyway. Particulate matter. The stuff the EPA doesn't even bother to check out here because the air is so pure. You should come and breathe it."

I wished it was that simple, but she was two hours away in the heart of Virginia, and it wasn't easy to get away to spend a weekend. "I'll get out there eventually," I promised, but I felt a pang somewhere in my shriveled heart at the word *eventually*. Gran was eighty, and spry as she'd been twenty years ago, but she wasn't going to be around forever. "I mean soon," I said. "I'll get out there soon. I worry about you alone in that big old house."

Gran gave a light laugh. "Don't worry about it, hon. My neighbor Brooke has been an absolute delight, keeping me so busy I don't have time to sit around feeling sorry for myself. She's why I called, actually."

I stifled a sigh as I started the car and pulled into traffic. There wasn't a thing that I didn't love about Gran, but if there was one thing I liked a tiny bit less than all her other stellar qualities, it was her relentless matchmaking. She did *not* let up, nor would she, she had informed me, until she saw her oldest unmarried grandchild happily settled. I braced myself for the sales pitch on this new neighbor. Gran had mentioned her before, trying to casually drop in that the young woman had moved in next door in the spring, and oh, by the way, had she mentioned how pretty she was?

But Gran surprised me with a totally different question. "How do I find a good lawyer for wills and things? Walter Sellers does them for everyone around here, but his wife Diane is always running her mouth about the details, and I don't need her airing mine for everyone."

I blinked, trying to follow the thread of the conversation. "Sorry, what does an estate lawyer have to do with your new neighbor?"

"Well, we've gotten to know each other so well that I've really come to love her like another grandchild. And you all are so busy with your lives, and I don't want this place to become a burden to you when I pass, nor do I want anyone to fight about it. So I'm thinking I may leave it to her. There's plenty of stocks and other things in the trust for the rest of you, but this will at least get the house out of everyone's hair."

My spidey senses tingled. Why was Gran suddenly wanting to leave her property to a woman who had only been her neighbor for a few months? I was one of the best investigators in Washington DC for a reason: I had excellent instincts and every one of them was screaming.

"Gran, everyone loves that place. And you don't have to worry that we'll fight about it. Just leave it in the trust like everything else. Landon will be a great executor. We all trust him." Landon was my younger brother, who had a steady temperament and a shiny law degree. "And can we please stop talking about what we're going to do with your stuff when you die? It's morbid."

I drove toward home, the usual urge to shower after doing surveillance work making me speed fast enough to upset the DC Metro police if they caught me.

"Death is only morbid to the young," she said, not sounding remotely subdued. "Death is a stranger to you, but I've finished up eight decades on this earth, and lately, he looks more like a familiar friend. I'm not at all worried about it. Don't plan to go soon, but 'soon' is relative these days. Just want to make sure everything is in good order, so I don't have that hanging over me while I enjoy whatever time I have left."

Impending death was her favorite tactic to guilt me into a visit. Every time it worked, I drove out to Creekville to find her in perfect health. I'd spend the whole weekend trying to convince her to let me take care of things around the property while fending off her efforts to spoil me. I always drove home feeling mildly annoyed but also way more relaxed than when I left.

But this was different. She wasn't dangling it over me to get me to come out. I tested the waters. "You know, Gran, I really haven't been out there in a few months. How about if I come out next weekend and fix some stuff around the place? I can put up that lattice for you."

She'd asked me to do it last summer, and I'd meant to get to it. More guilt prickled in my chest.

"Oh, it's fine, Ian-boy. It sounds like your job is keeping you plenty busy. I don't want to be a distraction. Just come out the next time you find yourself with some downtime. Brooke has been excellent company. She's keeping me young."

Now I was really worried. There were red flags and then there were six-foot neon letters spelling out S-C-A-M-M-E-R. But I couldn't let on that I was worried about the Brooke person or Gran would take offense that I didn't trust her judgment. Good thing navigating tricky undercurrents like this was my specialty.

"That's a relief, honestly, Gran," I said. "I do feel bad that work keeps me in the city so often. It's good to hear that you've got someone keeping an eye on you. This Brooke…what's her last name?" I kept my voice casual.

"Brooke Spencer," Gran said. "Loveliest young woman. She inherited Fred Sandberg's place next door. Her great-uncle, I think. He was withdrawn, kept to himself, but Brooke couldn't be sweeter."

The neon danger sign began to flash. This "sweet" Brooke had conveniently inherited an old man's property and now my grandmother was prepared to hand over hers as well? Not on my watch. My mouth pressed into a grim line. I spent all my time looking for the ways in which people cheated each other and exploited the systems that ordinary folks tried to live by. I could smell a swindle a mile away.

Well, 120 miles away, to be exact. Brooke Spencer was the kind of "sweet" that described rotten meat, and I could smell it from here. I'd gather as much information as I could without tipping off Gran, but I was getting to the bottom of this. It looked as if my weekend plans had just changed.

Gran was my newest client even if she didn't know I'd taken her case.

CHAPTER TWO

Brooke

I rocked back on my heels and shook out my shoulders. They were sore, but as I stared down the row of weeded tomato plants in Miss Lily's garden, I recognized it as the good kind of ache, the kind that came from an honest morning's work. I pulled off my gloves and was tucking them into the pocket in my garden tote when Miss Lily emerged through the French doors of her big Colonial-style house. Mansion?

I idly considered the question as I rose and waited for Miss Lily to cross the lawn—grounds?—to me so we could confer about the garden. It probably was a mansion, I conceded as I catalogued the home's features. It was only two stories, but long gracious wings extended from the center, and from the front, elegant windows welcomed guests arriving up the long drive. Also, the house sat on three acres, so that might qualify as more than just a yard. But Miss Lily herself was salt-of-the-earth, and it was hard to associate my gardening friend with the idea of something so grand as a mansion.

"Good afternoon, Miss Lily," I called.

"Didn't think I'd see you out here today, Brooke," the older woman answered as she drew near. She wore her favorite straw hat for working in the garden and carried her own well-used tote of garden tools. "Thought you were going into the school."

"I did for the morning, but they're not running the air conditioner until school starts in two weeks, so it got too hot and stuffy to get much done. I came home and did some more planning until I got too antsy and came out to weed. Come see." I beckoned Miss Lily to join me among the tomato plants. "I did the whole row."

"Well done," Miss Lily said. Her words were simple, but her proud smile warmed my heart. "You did a fine job."

"Thank you. When do you think they'll ripen?" I asked. "I can't wait to try one of your tomato sandwiches."

"It's one of the greatest pleasures in life, I assure you," Miss Lily said. "I can't believe you've gone this long without experiencing one." She bent down and inspected the orange fruit on a few of the plants. "Soon," she pronounced when she straightened. "Right around the time school starts."

"School" caused the same small flip in my stomach that it had since Lincoln High School had hired me as their new biology teacher for the fall. I'd worked hard to complete my credential and student teaching in just a year, but I hardly felt prepared to greet the 150 sophomores who would expect me to explain the fine points of genetics and taxonomy as Ms. Spencer the Science Teacher when school began.

Working on Uncle Fred's—no, *my* house—and helping Miss Lily in her garden helped keep my mind off the spectacular ways I might fail at my new career. Well, that and the mantra that I couldn't fail worse in this one than I had in my last one.

The familiar buzz of anxiety began to thrum in my chest, and I crouched by the next row, looking for more weeds to pull. Unfortunately, I'd taken care of this one a few days before and there wasn't much there.

"It's fine," Miss Lily said, waving me back up. "You've done more than enough for today. Why don't you come on up to the house and have some iced tea and visit?"

I wouldn't dream of hurting Miss Lily's feelings by turning her down. The woman had been my first and fastest friend in Creekville, a town that wasn't used to newcomers, but I felt a mighty urge to keep my hands busy so my mind couldn't wander into my school worries.

We all have to get through the learning curve. Everybody hates it, but you'll do fine. I'd repeated this strangely comforting piece of advice from my mentor teacher more times than I could count over the last week as school drew closer and closer to opening.

I didn't even realize I'd gotten lost in my own thoughts again until Miss Lily's silvery laugh broke in. "I can see you're going to be better off if we stay out here and work longer. But the squash needs our attention more than the beans. Let's go pick some."

"Really?" I darted to the end of the row. So far, I'd only been able to pick asparagus, bell peppers, and cucumbers. Every time Miss Lily let me harvest something new from the garden, it felt like Christmas. If Christmas were eighty degrees in the shade, that is. I hurried to the butternut squash and waited impatiently for Miss Lily to catch up.

"All right, hold your horses," Miss Lily said, another laugh in her voice. "They're not going anywhere." When she reached me beside the patch, she rewarded me with a big grin. "You know that these gardening lessons I'm giving you are an excuse to get you to do the work my back is too old for these days. You have been Tom Sawyered all summer long."

"I'm a willing sucker," I assured her. "I'm so glad you've let me do this. I feel more confident about starting my own garden next summer."

My place was much smaller, but it still sat on a half-acre, which was more than enough to plant a garden for one. But the very afternoon I'd met Miss Lily, I had mentioned how overwhelmed I was by renovating my uncle's aging home while tackling a garden too. She'd insisted that I come learn in her garden and take all the vegetables I wanted when they came in. My garden time with Miss Lily had become my favorite part of every day.

"You'll do fine," Miss Lily assured me, "but my garden is big enough for both of us. Didn't I tell you it would produce more than even the two of us could ever eat? Just work it with me again next spring. Now, let's pick some butternut squash. Mary makes a marvelous ravioli with it." Mary was her housekeeper and cook, and I had eaten at Miss Lily's table enough times to take this claim as gospel truth.

I did as Miss Lily directed, looking for squash that had grown to a size I might see at the farmer's market, then checking to make sure the color was uniform and showed no green spots on the rind.

"Make sure the skin isn't glossy either," Miss Lily said when I declared I'd found one. A few minutes later, I'd twisted and plucked three lovely butternuts from their vines and settled them in Miss Lily's basket.

"One of these should go home with you," Miss Lily said. "I would send you home with two, but Ian's coming tonight."

Ian. Her grandson. Miss Lily had spoken of him often. "I didn't know you were expecting him." I tried to keep my voice neutral, but despite Miss Lily's constant and clear pride in the guy, I wasn't impressed. I'd lived here five months already, and he hadn't come to visit his grandmother once.

"I'm not sure he even knows he's coming tonight, but he'll be here." Miss Lily wore a content smile.

A flicker of irritation toward Miss Lily's delinquent grandson fluttered through my chest. I was going to be even less impressed if Miss Lily went to bed disappointed tonight, let down again by Ian.

"So, tell me how school is going," Miss Lily said as we moved on to the green beans. "You feeling ready yet?"

I sighed. "I don't think I ever will. I was working in my classroom until after lunch, putting up a display of the metric system. And as I'm trying to staple butcher paper to the wall and think of cute puns, I'm thinking, 'Am I rearranging deck chairs while *The Titanic* sinks?' It won't do me any good to have clever bulletin boards if I freeze when those lab tables fill with students."

"You worry too much," Miss Lily said. "It's a cliché for a reason, but truly, those children want to know how much you care before they care how much you know. Stand up there and let your true self shine through and the rest will take care of itself."

Miss Lily had taught high school English for twenty-five years, so I wanted to believe this, but I didn't have that same twinkle in my eye that Miss Lily did, the one that invited whoever met her to come join her mischief. But I kept any further worries for myself. Burdening Miss Lily with them would be a poor repayment for all the kindness she had shown me in the last few months.

We worked in comfortable silence for a while, plucking crisp string beans and adding them to Miss Lily's basket. I had always liked green beans well enough, but they'd been a revelation when they'd ripened a couple of weeks ago and I'd brought my first batch home to stir fry straight from the vine. They'd popped and burst in my mouth, tasting like good earth and sunshine. "I can't imagine I'll love anything else from this garden as much as I love fresh beans."

"Wait until the sweet corn comes in next month. Nothing like an ear picked from the stalk then walked right into your kitchen and cooked." Miss Lily paused for a minute to pat at her glistening forehead with a hand-embroidered kerchief from the pocket of her gardening shirt. She glanced over the rows and smiled. "Gardens are how I get to know God, and how he shows his love for me. Sweet corn is proof."

I wished I had that same kind of faith, but I was glad I could at least borrow from Miss Lily's unshakeable belief. In gardens. In corn. In me. Every time Miss Lily spoke one of these little nuggets, it felt like my world steadied a bit. Not so long ago, I wouldn't have believed that I could ever regain the faith that people were fundamentally good and kind. But Miss Lily was slowly convincing me that at least one twinkly-eyed octogenarian on this earth was exactly that, and one was better than none.

Immediate annoyance followed the thought. *Her Ian is an absolute idiot for not coming to soak this all up.* Miss Lily had seven grandchildren, and two lived in other states, so it was understandable they didn't come to visit often. I had met most of the other five. Landon, Ian's brother fresh out of law school, had been by a few times. And Ian's cousins all visited to check on Miss Lily. But Ian, the one who lived closest, somehow could not be bothered to check on his grandmother.

The late afternoon sun was sliding toward dusk, and though Miss Lily turned her head at the sound of every car coming down the road with an air of expectation, there was still no sign of him as we gathered the last of the ripe beans.

Well, I couldn't do anything about my neighbor's flaky grandson, but I could at least try to manage Miss Lily's expectations, prepare her for yet another weekend where Ian the Idiot didn't show.

"It'll be dark soon," I noted, keeping my voice casual.

Miss Lily glanced at the sky. "Another hour at least. Though I should get this haul to Mary so she can start supper."

I wanted to say, "Tell her she's only cooking for you two," but I couldn't bear to squash Miss Lily's hopes so directly. Maybe my best bet was to give Miss Lily something else to look forward to. "What are we doing in the garden tomorrow?"

"*We* are doing nothing," Miss Lily told me. "I'll be transplanting the fall lettuce seedlings, but *you* have work to do on your house. You're going to be awfully busy when school starts. Better use your time while you have it. Are you working on the floors next?"

"Yes, ma'am." The sound of a riding mower cut through the quiet dusk as the teenage boy across the road set to work cutting his lawn. Better now than 8 AM, I decided. I raised my voice to be heard over the high whine of the engine. "I need to refinish the front room floors. But why don't you let me come over first thing in the morning and help you with the planting? I'd love to. I find it very satisfying."

"You're sweet, honey, but my grandson can do it. You get those floors taken care of. You'll feel better not having them to worry about."

I studied the elderly woman as she bent to examine a bell pepper plant, my irritation toward her grandson renewed. "I don't think he's coming, Miss Lily. No one who's ever eaten Mary's cooking would risk missing supper. If he's not here now, I think you'd better assume he won't be here at all."

I braced myself for the brightness to dim in Miss Lily's eyes, but her smile was steady as ever when she said, "You worry too much. He'll be here."

"Well, I hope so for your sake, Miss Lily. But just know if your grandson doesn't show up, I'll be here first thing in the morning to help you with the planting."

"That won't be necessary," a male voice said from the edge of the garden.

We both turned from the pepper plant, and Miss Lily's face brightened even more as she hurried down the row toward a tall man with dark blond hair, broad shoulders, and a big grin on his face. The mower had covered the sound of his arrival.

"Ian," Miss Lily cried as he hurried to meet her, his arms stretched out for her hug.

"Hey, Gran," he said, gathering her close to his chest. "How are you?"

"Completely copacetic now that you're here." She stepped back and waved me over.

I walked toward them slowly, taking the measure of this prodigal grandson.

"You cut it awfully close," Gran scolded him, but her tone held a world of love. "Mary will have supper on the table soon."

"Gran, how can you say I'm late when I didn't tell you I was coming? This was supposed to be a surprise. I didn't even tell Dad I was coming."

"Gran knows everything," she said. "Brooke, come here and meet Ian."

I took the last few steps to put myself in handshake range. Ian's wide grin for his Gran turned polite and cool as I extended my hand.

"Ian, this is my lovely neighbor, Brooke Spencer. She's going to be the new science teacher at Lincoln."

"Brooke," he said, his voice as cool as his smile. "Nice to meet you. I've heard so much about you."

"Same here," I said. *All of it good, and I don't believe a word of it.* I hoped the unspoken words showed up in my equally polite smile to him.

"You're off the hook," he said. "I'll help Gran with the planting tomorrow."

"How nice," I said. "I'm sure she'll appreciate having someone besides me coming over here every single day." I hoped he understood this subtext too: *I'm here because you never are.*

"I'm so pleased you two can finally meet," Miss Lily said, unaware of the undercurrents between me and my new nemesis, Ian the Idiot. "Brooke, why don't you go get cleaned up and come over for supper in half an hour? I'd love for two of my favorite people in the world to get to know each other."

Ian's brow creased slightly, but he didn't need to worry. I had no interest in crashing their dinner.

"That's kind, Miss Lily, but I have big plans for this squash tonight. Miss Mary doesn't need to stress about two extra mouths to feed. I need to get home and try my own kitchen experiment."

"That squash will keep forever," Miss Lily said. "You can experiment on it tomorrow. Mary just happened to cook a Mississippi roast, and there's plenty to go round. Ian and I will see you in a half hour."

"But I—"

"But nothing," Miss Lily said. "You don't want to hurt an old lady's feelings, do you?"

I sighed. "You're not playing fair."

"Child, you lost this argument the minute I mentioned Mary's roast and you know it. Now go on and get ready for supper."

I conceded defeat and gathered up my garden tote, the squash resting inside on a pile of green beans large enough to keep me fed for three meals in a row. I gave Miss Lily a warm smile and Ian a polite nod and headed back to my place.

Unlike the upscale neighborhood in McLean where I grew up, the properties here on the outskirts of town weren't separated by fences or even perfectly manicured hedgerows. It was as if people in the country each had enough land that they didn't feel the need to stake it out down to its last inch. The open yards allowed Miss Lily and me to wander between each other's homes freely, and it was one of the things I liked best about Creekville: everyone seemed to feel this way. Chances were when the kid across the street finished mowing his half-acre lawn, he'd glance around to see if any neighbors' grounds needed attention and cut it for them without a second thought.

I walked into the kitchen and unloaded my tote into the waiting wooden bowl on the counter, giving the pile of fresh string beans and squash one last look of longing. Mary's roast might be the only thing that could tempt me away because cooking up my small harvests had become one of my favorite parts of the day. Making small talk with strangers…not so much, however good I'd been at it in my old life.

Still, Miss Lily had issued her orders, and I would obey her because she was the grandmother I'd always wished I had, and I could appreciate her even if Ian the Idiot could not.

CHAPTER THREE

Ian

I watched Brooke go, analyzing my reaction to her. I'd been startled by her appearance. It's not that I'd expected her to dress the part in sunglasses and a trench coat, but neither had I expected the fresh-faced prettiness of a woman straight out of one of my mom's Land's End catalogues.

I should have. My training was better than that. Sometimes corruption advertised itself in the faces of people who had indulged themselves too long in hard living. Rich foods and expensive drugs made for soft bodies and worn faces. But far more often, the most corrupt people were the ones you didn't see coming, the kinds who looked unassuming and ordinary. Pleasant, even. It was what made them so dangerous.

"I'm so glad you came," Gran said again, squeezing me around the waist, and I returned the love.

"Me too, but how did you know I was coming?"

She smiled up at me. "Grandma instincts are as good as motherly ones about things like this. Now come on into the house. Let's get you settled, then you can tell us all about the capi-*dull* over dinner."

I grinned at Gran's unrepentant disdain for the nation's capital. She'd always said the only thing more useless than a square tire was a politician. I couldn't disagree, but the very consistency of their self-absorption and naked thirst for power enabled me to make a very nice living, so viva la politicians, the more craven, the better.

We returned to the house, and I inhaled deeply as we stepped through the French doors into the large, open room she called the "gathering room." The familiar scent of gardenias, soft but distinct, wafted to me. I didn't know if the house smelled like Gran or vice versa, but I could never smell gardenias without it transporting me straight back to this room. It was the figurative and literal center of the home, where our family gathered at Thanksgiving for every minute that wasn't spent in the formal dining room feasting on the spread Mary cooked up. We all lounged in the gathering room while the grandkids played at one end, the sports fans watched football at the other end, and everyone else spread on the sofas and comfy armchairs in between, laughing and catching up. It *had* been too long since I'd come to visit.

"It's been too long," Gran said, echoing my identical thought. How did she do that? "But I'm glad you're here. Now run up and put your things in your room while I check on dinner."

I fetched my weekend bag from my BMW convertible. It had been forever since I'd taken it for a joyride. I spent most of my time driving a sensible hybrid painted a color somewhere between beige and silver, the perfect car to blend into any neighborhood. The BMW was my gift to myself three years ago on my thirtieth birthday, a luxury for when I was on my own time, but I'd had so little time to put any mileage on it that it looked brand new.

I traded my wrinkled gray golf shirt for a collared button up appropriate for Gran's country club casual dinner aesthetic, splashed cold water over my face, and headed downstairs.

"Hey, Mary." I popped my head into the kitchen to smile at the woman tossing a salad. She was probably near sixty, but her plump face had a softness to it that always made her seem ten years younger, especially when she beamed at me.

"Ian!" she said, setting down the salad tongs and clapping her hands in delight. "It's so good to see you."

I sniffed the air. "All you have to do is cook this every Friday, and you'll lure me out here every weekend."

She laughed and held her arms out for a hug. I stepped into the room, happy to oblige. "You're too skinny," she complained.

"No good food in DC," I said.

She released me and shooed me toward the door. "Go find your grandmother. Dinner is almost ready."

I obeyed, wandering into the gathering room where Gran stood beside the drinks cart. "Bourbon?" she asked.

"Sounds great." I accepted the glass and then sat beside her on the sofa to wait for the gold digger to arrive. "So, tell me about this new neighbor of yours," I said, taking a sip. She might be a poor judge of neighbors, but she had great taste in whiskey.

"Brooke is a sweetheart, isn't she?" Gran said.

"Mmm," I offered, a noncommittal sound that she could interpret however she liked.

"She's been a breath of fresh air around here. It's good for Mary and me to have her youth and energy in the house. She's smart as a whip and funny too." She eyed me over the rim of her martini glass as she took a casual sip. "And pretty."

Gran was never as subtle as she liked to think, and I ignored the bait. "Hope she comes soon. I'm starving." *To know what she's up to*, I silently amended. And for Mary's roast. Only a fool wouldn't be salivating over the aroma drifting from the kitchen.

The French doors stood open, and Brooke chose that moment to step in from the falling darkness outside. Speak of the devil and she shall appear. She'd changed to a sleeveless white dress that made her lightly tanned skin kind of glowy. If she'd put on any makeup, she'd used a very light hand. She was projecting the effortless dewiness that Washington socialites spent thousands at the high-end spas outside of the Beltway to achieve.

"Hey," she said, gliding toward Gran to drop a kiss on her cheek.

She waved Gran back down when she rose to prepare Brooke a drink. "I'll get it. You relax."

She poured herself vodka and tonic with a splash of cranberry, navigating the drink cart with ease, like she'd done it often. She knew exactly where to find everything, no hesitation as she reached for the ice tongs or seltzer water.

"When did you say you moved here, Brooke?" I asked.

"In February," she said without looking up.

Not quite five months ago. That was no time at all in a place like Creekville where most families had lived for a minimum of three generations. How had she weaseled into Gran's life so quickly? It didn't smell right. At all.

"Do you like it here?" I asked, trying to draw her out. I needed a better sense of her so I could look for the cracks that would expose her.

"I do," she said, taking a seat in the armchair opposite us, her drink in hand. "It's a nice antidote to the way I grew up."

It was a helpful clue and gave me a direction to follow. If she'd grown up opposite of Gran, that meant poor. The quiet wealth of Gran's home and property would be dizzying to someone who came from less. Everything about Gran's home was understated and welcoming, but there was no mistaking that a house of this size on grounds this large, all of it beautifully maintained, spoke of deep pockets.

I didn't care about that kind of stuff. Not really. Not beyond liking that I could buy my dream car and afford a decent condo. Gran and Gramps had raised their three kids to work hard and value what they earned by their own hands, and my parents had passed that to me and my three siblings. One day, when I slowed down long enough to marry and have kids of my own, I'd teach them the same thing.

But I currently worked too hard to slow down and figure out the dating and marriage thing. Besides, in my line of work, I saw way too many cheaters. But Brooke, she'd gone one rung lower to gold digger, if I didn't miss my guess. And I never, ever missed my guess. My work depended on it.

Mary appeared in the doorway to confirm what our noses were telling us. "Dinner's ready, y'all."

I rose and offered Gran my arm as my mom had taught me to do when I was little, and she settled her small hand into the crook of my elbow and led the way to the breakfast nook. She preferred to eat there instead of the formal dining room unless the party was large.

As we settled around the oak table, I continued to monitor Brooke closely without appearing to do so. It was a necessary skill for an investigator, the ability to observe carefully without making the subject feel like she was under a microscope.

I wondered first at her age. She didn't look a day over twenty-five, but she carried herself with the confidence of someone with more life experience, which made me stick with my original guess of thirty. Next, I listened for the way she spoke. She didn't have a discernible accent, but she was articulate in a way that suggested a good education. That or she was a gifted mimic of educated people. I'd seen it go both ways. She had to have at least a bachelor's degree to also hold a teaching credential, but I'd uncover all these things when I did an Internet search after dinner.

The average American would be appalled by how easy it was to examine the minutiae of their lives with a visit to a few databases, but it definitely made my job easier.

Gran had chosen a cabernet for the roast, and I poured a glass of wine and hid a smile behind it. Poor Brooke. She might be good enough to fool lonely senior citizens with her sweet smile and interested questions, but she couldn't fool my Google skills.

"How's the house coming along?" Gran asked her.

"Slowly," Brooke said with a sigh. I was content to let Gran steer the conversation. It gave me more opportunity to observe my subject. "It's a great house," she explained to me. "But I don't think my uncle did a single update the whole time he owned it. Tomorrow I start the floors." She followed that with a grimace. "It's a big job, but it's cheaper to rent the equipment and do it myself than hire a contractor."

She was very good. She was too smart to come out and say, "I sure wish someone would give me the money to do this." Instead, she planted subtle hints about the scope of the work and the expense of the undertaking.

Gran shot Brooke an admiring smile. "This one is convinced there's nothing she can't conquer with the right YouTube tutorial."

"Oh, it's never just one," Brooke said, with a shake of her head and a small laugh. "You have to watch at least ten, and the correct answer lies somewhere in the middle. You start to see a consensus about a few things, and then you can piece together an approach that will get the job done."

"Ian is pretty handy," Gran said. "My John made all our kids help keep this place running, assigning them to shifts with the groundskeeper during the week and overseeing their chores himself on the weekend."

Gramps had been a gruff old man for as long as I could remember, a result of him presiding over the law school at the University of Virginia for so many years. "Lawyers make me cranky," Gramps had told me one summer when I visited. "Don't be one." Somehow, I'd still ended up working with lawyers anyway, and unsurprisingly, Gramps had been exactly right about them.

"I'll send Ian over to help tomorrow," Gran said in a tone that made it clear she'd made up her mind.

Foolish Brooke attempted to argue with her. "Oh, you don't need to do that. I've already remodeled an entire bathroom with the help of YouTube and calling Grace at the hardware store in town every time I have a question. I'm sure they'll both get me through another Saturday without much trouble."

"It's fine," I said. "I'm happy to. My dad raised me the way Gramps raised him, and I'm handy as advertised." Normally, I might look forward to sleeping in on a weekend visit to Gran, followed by a round of golf, and then a leisurely afternoon on the back porch with her. But I was here to assess the threat Brooke posed, and a home improvement project was the perfect cover to spend more time with her. By tomorrow morning, I'd have gone deep down the Internet, and I'd have plenty of questions for her while we worked.

"He's fine. You see?" Gran said, her tone smacking of "I told you so." "He's a good boy. Happy to help."

We passed the rest of dinner chatting about Brooke's extensive (and expensive-sounding) renovation plans. When Mary came to clear the dinner dishes, Brooke placed her napkin on the table as though she were done and earned herself a stern look and a headshake from Gran.

"Not so fast, young lady. You still need dessert."

"I couldn't possibly make room," Brooke protested. "Mary is too good a cook. I'm full to bursting."

"Oh, fine then," Gran said, leaning back. "But it's a shame to pass up fresh ice cream made with peaches straight from Jimmy Lowe's trees."

Brooke promptly dropped her napkin on her lap.

"Smart girl," Gran said, grinning.

By the time we polished off the peach ice cream and butter cake Mary had made, even I was sure another crumb would make me burst. I sympathized when Brooke pushed back from the table with a groan.

"All right, I really need to go," she said, rising. "I'm going to have to roll myself home, but I definitely need a good night's sleep before I tackle the floors tomorrow. Good night, Miss Lily. I hope you dream of peaches. I know I will."

"I might be stuck here," Gran confessed lazily from her chair. "Mary surely outdid herself. Ian, why don't you walk Brooke home then come help your overindulgent grandmother up from the table."

"I'll be fine," Brooke protested. "You stay and take care of Miss Lily."

"Sorry," I said, already rising. "But I never disobey Gran."

Gran shooed us away with a laugh, and I walked Brooke to the patio doors. But when I stepped out behind her, prepared to see her across Gran's well-lit grounds to her unlit yard, she turned and held up her hand.

"No need to walk me home," she said. "Miss Lily worries too much."

"It's dark," I said. "I don't mind."

"I do. You came here to visit her, and she's been waiting a long time for that."

Disapproval ran through her tone.

What did I care if she banged her shin or bumped into an oak or two in her stubbornness? She was right; I was here for Gran, and I'd have plenty of time to dig the truth out of Brooke tomorrow. "All right, then. Have a good night."

She gave me another of her polite nods and headed for her uncle's place, melting into the shadows as she finally crossed Gran's property line.

I watched the spot where she'd disappeared for a long time, considering what I'd learned from my observations. First and foremost, it was easy to see how an astute judge of character like Gran had been taken in by this wholesome-looking woman. She had an easiness about her that appealed to Gran's good humor and warmth, and if I hadn't known she was sketchy, she might have charmed me too.

But I *did* know, and I noticed more warning signs. Her subtle changes in topic whenever Gran's conversation veered toward anything about Brooke's life before two years ago. How she'd touched on her childhood a few times in the most general terms when I'd shared my own stories about summers at Gran's. Nothing came up from college or after. It was as if her adult life didn't exist before eighteen months ago, when she'd started her teaching credential.

Why the gap? She didn't fill it even when I asked questions about what she'd been up to between high school graduation and staying with her uncle before his death.

Whatever secrets Brooke Spencer was hiding, they wouldn't stay that way for long.

CHAPTER FOUR

Brooke

The pounding on my door started at 8:30 AM. It was loud and insistent, even over the high whine of the floor sander the hardware store owner, Grace, had delivered to me at 7 AM before going in to open for business.

I slid my safety goggles up to rest on my head and headed for the door, wrinkling my nose behind the mask I'd worn to keep out all the sawdust. I had no doubt it was Ian the Idiot standing on the other side of the door, but I didn't want his help. I'd send him back to Miss Lily so I could get back to sanding. And there was just So. Much. Sanding.

Ian's eyebrows flew up when I pulled open the front door. I barely refrained from an eyeroll. Who had he expected to answer? The ghost of Great Uncle Fred?

"Hey," I said without ceremony. I'd almost found my rhythm with the sander and I didn't want to lose it.

"Good morning. Looks like you already got started. Are you renovating or doing mad science?" He pointed at the safety goggles.

Now it was my turn to raise an eyebrow. "I've been at it for over an hour. Sanding, that is. I don't start experiments until next week."

He blinked at me and looked confused.

I pointed a thumb at myself. "Science teacher, remember?"

His expression cleared. "Biology, right? I thought experiments were more for chemistry."

"Congratulations, you know your high school science. And I have good news for you: you're off the hook. There's only one sander, and I've got it down, so you can go hang out with Miss Lily, guilt-free." I hadn't enjoyed him at dinner the night before, the way he watched me so closely, like he was trying to figure out what made me tick. He'd tried to be so smooth in his questions, but I'd had too much experience with other smooth operators to find his interest flattering. It felt intrusive, and I had no interest in being under his magnifying glass again, like I was one of his suspects. I started to close the door, but he stuck his foot inside it.

I stared down at his sneaker then back at him and gave him the teacher stare I'd been practicing. I narrowed my eyes slightly in a way that I hoped demanded, "Just what do you think you're doing?" but with no words.

He didn't move the sneaker. "If you think she's going to let me back in the house without putting in my work over here, you don't know her. If you don't let me in, I'm going to have to wander out of her view for a few hours, and you're going to have to tell her you let me help you. So maybe just let me come in and do some sanding?"

I didn't have time for this. I only had the sander for one day, and I didn't want to waste any more time arguing with him about it. I turned away from him and left him to decide whether he wanted to follow or not. "Shut the door behind you," I called over my shoulder, and I didn't care if "behind" him was him coming or going. But the door clicked shut as I resettled my goggles, and the creak of his footsteps followed right behind.

"I've never been inside Fred's house before." He stood at the edge of the dining room where I'd decided to start. I planned to turn it into a library, and if I botched the floor horribly, it would be the perfect place to put a nice, thick rug so nobody ever knew.

"Like I said last night, it has good bones. I'm mostly in here doing cosmetic surgery, not orthopedic, thank goodness." I flipped the switch on the sander but before I could begin the steady grind along the oak grain, Ian waved his arms to get my attention. "Is this charades?" I asked, cutting the motor.

"Just wondering where you'd like me to start," he said.

"I don't know," I said. "There's one sander. That's what I'm trying to explain. I don't have anything for you to do."

"I could supervise."

My eyes narrowed again until the corner of his lips twitched. It kind of sucked as a joke. "I guess you can sweep up the sawdust." There. *Slink home in defeat, buddy.*

But he only nodded. "Sure. Broom?"

I had a shop broom in the laundry room, but I fetched a short-handled brush and dustpan instead. "Here you go." I thrust it at him with a cheerful smile. Not that he could see it through the dust mask I didn't bother removing.

I fired up the sander and set to work, moving along the boards, going with the grain of the wood at the steady pace that Hardware Grace and a dozen YouTube videos had advised. Ian knelt without a word and began sweeping the small area I'd already sanded, but it was only a couple of minutes before he started coughing, and two more before he set the brush down, mouthed something to me I didn't catch, and walked out.

"I win," I muttered.

I wished the sander weren't quite so loud so I could listen to music or a podcast while I worked, but I settled for the company of my own thoughts, imagining all the books I'd fill the shelves with.

I'd organize them by frequency of use. The cookbooks definitely would go at eye level on the shelf nearest the kitchen. The classics from high school would go on the highest shelf. I wasn't likely to pull those down again.

I was deep into mentally organizing my shelf of book club favorites when a movement out of the corner of my eye startled me into a yelp. The sander went skittering diagonally a few inches before I steadied my grip.

"Sorry," Ian said, when I cut the power. "Didn't mean to scare you. I ran into town and rented a floor edger. Figured it would be more helpful if I did that than sweeping, although I'm happy to do that when we're done."

"Okay," I said, eyeing the shiny chrome machine he'd set on the floor beside him. "Good idea, I guess."

Then I crouched to examine the damage I did when he'd surprised me. I sighed. It wasn't good, but luckily, it was near the corner furthest from either door. The shelves might even cover the short strip I'd sanded against the grain. If not, I'd shelve the books over here that people would least like to read. Maybe that was where the classics could go.

"Something wrong?" he asked.

I straightened. "I jumped when you came in. It sent the sander off track."

He took a step toward me like he was going to examine the damage himself, but I waved him off. "I got it."

He nodded and scanned the twenty feet of boards I'd sanded behind me. "Looks good though."

He didn't need to sound so surprised. I didn't dignify that with an acknowledgment, merely moved the sander over and started its high whine again, content as it ate through years of old varnish, grinding down the old oak just enough to smooth out the divots. The floors weren't in terrible condition, but they'd been stained in the medium gold color that had been so popular decades ago. I had a vision of dark floors to complement the pale putty-colored paint I'd used on the walls. Hardware Grace had told me about a contractor who could build me custom bookcases, and I imagined them in white. I wasn't a gifted designer, but I could copy the pages I liked in the Pottery Barn catalog as well as the next person. So far, I liked the way the vibe in the house had shifted after I'd repainted the forest green with inviting neutrals.

Now that Ian was underfoot again, I was grateful for the noisy motor. I might not be able to hear my podcasts, but neither did I have to keep up a conversation with him.

We worked in silence for a couple of hours, and I found a groove, going faster and watching the sanded floor emerge behind me in long, satisfying strips.

Still, by the time I called a break to give my arms a rest from the vibrations, only about a quarter of the floor was done. Ian had finished half his section, but then again, he was only focused on the edges. Better him than me, I conceded. I hated the tedious finish work of edges and corners.

"I'm going to grab some water," I said. "Can I get you some?"

"Sure, that would be great." But when I walked into the kitchen, he followed me instead of waiting for me to return. I stifled a sigh and filled a glass for him from the dispenser in the fridge door. It was shiny and black, a sharp contrast to the beige and brown oven, but Uncle Fred's fridge had failed shortly after I'd moved in, so I'd replaced it with a new model.

"Haven't tackled anything in here yet, huh?"

"Brilliant deduction." Then, feeling petty for being sarcastic when he'd been helping me all morning, I tried again. "Eventually, I'll upgrade everything in here, but the kitchen is my lowest priority. It's the biggest project, and I'll have to contract out."

"Expensive too."

What was it with this guy and his constant comments on the cost of things? "Yeah. It's not just that. My mother was constantly remodeling rooms in our house growing up, and I'll survive a kitchen remodel better if I have places to escape to in the rest of the house. Sometimes you need to get away from the workers and the dust and noise. I need to get through this first school year and do this next summer when I'm off and I can supervise."

I handed Ian his water and turned my back on the kitchen in favor of returning to the dining room and admiring my progress again. It was coming along. Good little sander. Totally worth the rental. Except...I crouched to examine the sandpaper.

Ugh. It was wearing thin and needed changing. I bit back a mild curse. Well, it looked like I might need Ian's help after all. I glanced over my shoulder to see if he'd come in from the kitchen and found him leaning against the doorway, studying me.

"What?" I asked.

"Everything okay with the sander?"

"No. I have to switch the paper out, and I think it's going to be a two-person job."

"Happy to help." He set down his glass and walked over. "Haven't worked with a floor sander before. Do you know how to do this?"

"I think so. I have to turn it over to switch it out. I was kind of hoping you would do the turning over part." It was a heavy machine. It had taken both Grace and I to get it into the house this morning.

"I got this." He gave me a cheeky bicep flex. "They don't call me Muscles for nothing."

I didn't smile, instead letting my gaze slip away and mumbling something about getting the new sheet. His arms were annoyingly impressive.

I fetched the sandpaper from the foyer where I'd left the box sitting beside the front dining room entrance. *Library* entrance. I was allowed to call it by its new name.

I dawdled while pulling out the new sheet. Ian had been poking fun at himself with the flexing, and I'd always gone for brain over brawn, but something about the way the cotton of his worn blue T-shirt had pulled over his arms had made my cheeks warm. I needed a second to collect myself. I'd been man-deprived for a long time, but I wasn't fixing the problem with Ian.

When I walked back into the library, he had the sander flipped over on the floor.

I crouched beside him. "I think we loosen that circular nut from the plate, pull off the old sheet, and put the new sheet on."

"Let's do it."

I took a stab at it, but it wouldn't budge. I frowned and tried again. "Righty-tighty, lefty-loosey, right?" I asked.

"Yeah. Want me to try?"

"No, I got it." But after a few more attempts and a very sore thumb and index finger, I conceded that I did not, in fact, "have it." "All right,

I need to go find my wrench." I wasn't sure which tool I would need for the job, but so far, plunking down my toolbox by everything I'd had to fix then pulling each tool out one by one and holding it up to the problem had helped me repair a lot of things in the house.

I climbed to my feet and headed for the laundry room where I kept the toolbox on the washing machine. It was as good a place as any to keep it since the washer didn't work. I'd been using it to store cans of sample paint and washing my clothes at Miss Lily's house.

I stared at the tools for a while, picking them up and considering each before I settled on the three I thought would most likely suit the job, but when I returned to the dining—*library*, Ian was sitting beside the sander with the used sandpaper in his lap.

"You got it," I said, annoyed with myself for being relieved that I wouldn't have to figure it out after all.

"I did." But he looked sheepish. His bangs were almost long enough to fall into his eyes, like he was overdue for a haircut, and he brushed them out of the way. "There may have been a complication."

"What kind of complication?"

"When I pulled out the screw, it slipped and rolled away. I was about to look for it."

I scanned the floor. "Which way did it roll?" A silver screw wouldn't be too hard to spot, unless...

Ian pointed to the thick sawdust coating the sanded area. "That way."

"Of course it did," I muttered. Rule one of home improvement was that nothing ever went right, and rule two was that it always went wrong in the least convenient way possible.

"Sorry about that. Don't worry, I'll find it."

I glanced down at my watch. "It's lunchtime. You're off the hook. You can report to Miss Lily that you've done the time. I'll sweep up the dust and find the screw."

"No, really I—"

"You've done enough," I said, keeping my voice even. It was no surprise to discover I'd have been better off switching it out by myself the hard way. Story of my life.

"I'll find it." He tugged off his sneakers.

"What are you doing?"

"I'm going to shuffle through it barefoot. That's how I'll find it."

A smile tugged at my lips in spite of myself. I had to give him points for trying. "All right. You start at that end doing it your way," I pointed to the far corner, "and I'll start at this end doing it mine."

"What's your way?"

"Don't worry about it." I fetched the shop broom from the laundry room and smirked when his eyebrows rose and looked from the short-handled broom I'd given him to the full-sized broom I now carried. But neither of us said anything as we set to work, him carefully stepping barefoot across the sawdust, me sweeping it up in short, brisk strokes as I watched for the screw.

"Have you done all the renovations yourself so far?" he asked after a minute.

"Yes. That's why it's going so slow. I do a lot of things the hard way first."

"It looks good," he said.

"You don't know what it looked like before."

"Do I need to have seen it to think that it looks good now?"

I rested against the broom handle. "I guess not. But you'd know how far it's really come even if it feels like it's taking forever most weeks."

"Are you on a deadline or something?"

I shook my head and went back to sweeping. "No. I'm just the impatient type, I guess."

He shuffled a few more steps before asking another question. "Were you close to your uncle?" Puffs of dust rose with each step.

"Not until shortly before he died." Uncle Fred had been so good to me, giving me a place to live for a little while. When I was young, he'd kept a squirrel feeder in his backyard that had delighted me with its constant traffic on my visit, and each year on my birthday, he'd sent a card with a squirrel on it, a crisp twenty-dollar bill tucked inside with a note to spend it stocking up on nuts.

Maybe that was why I'd thought of him when I'd found myself

with a sudden desperate need to escape from DC and the scandal erupting around me. He'd been kind enough to offer me shelter from the storm, no questions asked.

I went back to sweeping, but Ian, unlike Uncle Fred, was chock full of questions.

"He didn't have any kids?" he asked.

"No."

"Nice of him to leave his place to you."

That wasn't a question, so I didn't answer. He really *was* nosy. Must be a job hazard. He drew a breath like he was about to ask another question, but since they all seemed focused on my past and that was my least favorite topic, I decided to change the subject to him.

"So how'd you get into detective work?" I asked. "That's what you do, right?"

"I guess you could call it that. That makes me think of police though. My work is…messier than that."

"Messy how?"

"I don't have to follow the same rules."

I stopped sweeping again. "That doesn't sound at all ominous."

He laughed, revealing straight white teeth. He had Miss Lily's smile. "I'm one of the good guys."

"Are you though?" I'd dealt with my fair share of high-powered law firms. "Fair" wasn't a word I would use to describe their tactics or their results.

"The people I investigate don't think so. But my work probably wouldn't bother them so much if I weren't always catching them misbehaving."

"You still didn't say how you got into your line of work. And why do it for a law firm? Why not the FBI or CIA? Don't most guys with a sense of duty end up working for the intelligence services? Although maybe you're not that into duty." It still annoyed me that he made his grandmother pine for his visits so often.

He stopped shuffling. "What makes you say that?"

"I've met Landon and the other grandchildren several times, but this is the first time I've seen you come around."

"My job is demanding," he said, sending up an extra big puff of sawdust. "It's harder to get away."

"That's interesting, because Landon still managed to make it out to spend a Sunday afternoon with Miss Lily, and I think he's a first-year associate and therefore has no life outside of the firm, right?"

He didn't say anything to that. Finally, he said, "I went to law school."

"Excuse me?" What did that have to do with his delinquent grandson status?

"You asked why I worked for the law firm instead of going into law enforcement. It's because I went to law school at Georgetown and got hired by Fleming, Roth, and Schill."

I knew who they were. I'd even had some dealings with them in my old job. Ian must have been top of his class to get hired as a first-year associate.

"But you don't work for them as a lawyer, so..."

"I discovered the part I liked best about the job was the research. I didn't like having to recruit new clients. I hated preparing briefs and motions. But the research? I could do that all day. And the most fun was when I got to work with the firm's investigator to track down reluctant witnesses or clear up fuzzy details in their statements. So I decided to do all the fun parts of the job and skip the paperwork." He tilted his head and met my eyes. "Did I mention I'm very good at what I do?"

It sounded less like a brag and more like...a warning? I had no idea what he was trying to warn me against, but it didn't matter. He wasn't interrogating me anymore, and that was all I'd been after.

A grunt from Ian drew my attention as he bent down and fished something from beneath his foot. "Found it," he said, straightening and holding it up, a slight wince on his face. I only *sort of* hoped it had found the soft part of his sole.

"Thanks," I said, going to fetch it from him. "I've got it from here. I could point you to my first-aid kit, but I have a feeling Miss Lily would enjoy fussing over you, so why don't you go on back and let her take care of your foot?"

I stooped to secure the new sandpaper to the sander. He was silent for a moment, then offered a quiet, "Bye" as he fetched his shoes and socks and padded out the front door. I didn't answer him.

It was a poor demonstration of the manners my mother had drilled into me since childhood, but his explanation of his job had finally clarified the uncomfortable feeling I'd had since he'd shown up: he was part of the establishment machine that had chewed me up and spit me out, broken, two years ago.

I'd left people like him behind for a reason, and I didn't like him popping up in my peaceful Creekville bubble. Since moving in, I'd wished for Miss Lily's sake that the prodigal grandson would drag himself home, but now I couldn't wait until he disappeared again.

He'd have to head back tomorrow, probably after Sunday dinner, if Miss Lily could convince him to stay that long. Miss Lily and I had taken to eating Sunday dinners together with Mary lately, but I would plead a headache tomorrow and make it up to Miss Lily later. It wouldn't even be a lie, because that's exactly what Ian was: a headache I couldn't wait to be rid of.

CHAPTER FIVE

Ian

I hobbled home, gave my foot a good wash, and dabbed on some antibacterial junk. I'd gotten some interesting wounds "in the line of duty" as an investigator, but I wasn't so sure this one would pay off in the end like others had. I'd gone over to Brooke's this morning with a determination to fill the giant gap in her online history, and I hadn't left with any more information than when I'd arrived.

I settled back on the guest bed and pulled out my laptop to review her file, a list of links to all the places I'd found her digital footsteps. Her social media hadn't told me much. The last few months, she'd mostly documented her renovation and gardening projects, no mention of anything personal. Even prior to that, her pictures were largely of places and things, not people. She took pictures of buildings she found interesting, sunsets, and lots of plants and flowers.

Her Linked-In profile told me far more, but mostly because of what it left out. I'd started at the beginning, which was simply a mention of high school. Based on her graduation date, I was correct about her age. She was thirty. It didn't take long to find a copy of the yearbook one of her nostalgic classmates had scanned into a McLean High School Class of 2009 Facebook group. McLean, Virginia was one of DC's most affluent suburbs with McMansions occupied by top military brass and actual mansions owned by foreign ambassadors and DC lobbyists.

So she had come from money. Or at least from a solidly upper middleclass upbringing. Interesting. How did she go from that to scamming?

Her senior portrait listed her activities beneath it. Model UN, Key Club, class secretary, National Merit Scholar, president of Girls in STEM. I traced her to college at UVA. We would probably have overlapped on campus by about a year. Not that I expected to have crossed paths with her at a college of 21,000. She'd been in a sorority, one more noted for service than partying. She'd taken an extra semester to graduate then joined a public policy think tank in DC. She'd stayed there a year then worked as a staffer in the office of her representative to the Virginia legislature for two more. Next came her credential program and her new job as the biology teacher at Lincoln High School.

But it was the three blank years between her job at the delegate's office and her teaching credential that interested me most. That hole suggested someone who wished to forget or hide a significant part of her life. Those were always, *always* the very most interesting and telling parts. Especially because her stay with her uncle, Fred Sandberg, fell during that window. So why was it unaccounted for in all her public profiles?

On paper, her education and career would lead me to expect a polished Virginia socialite, not the woman who had opened her door this morning in denim overalls, her light brown hair in two braids with a fine film of sawdust clinging to it. But then, I'd seen a glimpse of that socialite last night in her ease with Gran, comfortable in her gathering room and at her table, etiquette on point, not remotely overawed by the subtle luxury of her surroundings.

What is hiding in that job gap, Brooke Spencer?

I'd know soon. Last night I'd only begun to search. Today began the dig.

I opened my email and sent my first message to ferret out the secrets she wasn't telling. By the time I drove home Sunday night, I knew which threads to pull.

Monday morning, I called in my assistant, a middle-aged woman named Sherrie who'd joined the firm as a paralegal but had been bitten by the same bug that had drawn me to investigation. She was turning into a skilled investigator in her own right. Her self-described "average mom vibe" made it easy to fly under everyone's radar, from hotel clerks to security guards. She could get into the most elite gated neighborhoods in Georgetown if she slapped the magnet for a catering business on the side of her minivan.

"I have a job for you," I said as she settled in across the desk from me. "Off the books."

Sherrie's eyebrows rose. I'd never made that request from her, but she only nodded.

"Lay it on me, boss."

"This is of a personal nature, and I'll pay you the firm's rate, but you'll still need to bill your regular hours for the partners."

"That's fine," she said. "My schedule is light for the next two weeks until my kids go back to school. I can put in some off-book overtime."

"All right. I need you to monitor this woman." I slid a photo of Brooke that I'd shot from my window while she helped Gran pick more green beans on Sunday. "Her name is Brooke Spencer. She mysteriously inherited a valuable property from a great-uncle she had no prior relationship to, and now she's in the middle of expensive renovations after no visible source of income for the last two years. She's about to start a job as a public school teacher. On paper, she shouldn't be able to afford any of this."

"So I'm doing a general tail and looking for patterns that don't fit with a school teacher's lifestyle."

"Exactly. I'm also going to text you the serial number for the tracking device I put on her car." Sherrie didn't bat an eye. Most of the stereotypes about PIs in books and movies were a joke, but every now and then even Hollywood got it right. It was expensive to pay someone by the hour to stake out a suspect unless you knew you would be catching them in the act of wrongdoing. In the early part of an investigation, a tracking device on a vehicle was a much more efficient way to establish patterns. It took a few days, but suspects always gave themselves away.

Brooke was considerate enough to do it on the first afternoon.

"I got something, boss," Sherrie said, ducking into my office. "She just pinged at 21305 Glen Forest Drive in Richmond."

I pulled up the address and gave a low whistle. "Why is innocent Brooke Spencer, high school science teacher, driving an hour to visit Highmark Wealth Management?" It was one of the largest wealth management firms on the East Coast with branches in most major cities. They wouldn't touch a client with less than a million in assets.

"If you've taught me anything, it's to follow the money," Sherrie said. "If you find the answer to that, you find the answer to everything."

"You've been paying attention," I said. "All right, good work. Keep watching her. Let me know if you see any other red flags."

"You got it." Sherrie went back to her own desk, and I stared at the link on the screen for Highmark. I didn't need to read up on them. Many of the firm's clients also had their assets managed by Highmark. Many of their *wealthy* clients. Nothing in Brooke's work history suggested that she'd been able to earn the kind of money she'd need for Highmark to bother with her.

Family money, then? I turned up her parents' info quickly enough. Her mother was from Charlottesville as Brooke had explained, and she had a current law license, but she didn't seem to have practiced law since 1992. Brooke's father worked for a defense contractor. I located their house on Google maps, a comfortable suburban home in McLean's best school district purchased when Brooke was seven. Even though their 3500 square foot home would cost upward of a million in today's market, it still didn't speak to the kind of family wealth that would merit attention from Highmark.

I spent another hour pulling on internet threads, further scouring for other traces of her, but didn't turn up anything new. That meant it was time to do some old school sleuthing. I wanted to retrace the steps of Brooke's life to see if I could find the point where a woman from an upper middleclass family became a predatory con artist. I started with her volunteer service listed in her yearbook profile at the Landsdowne Senior Center.

"Hello," I said to the receptionist who answered the phone. "I'm calling to do a reference check on a former volunteer. Can I speak to your human resources director?"

"Sure, hold please," said the young-sounding guy on the other end.

A minute later, a woman's voice came on the line. "Landsdowne Human Resources, how can I help you?"

"Hello. I'm calling for a reference check on one of your volunteers we're considering hiring."

"Name, please?"

"Brooke Spencer."

"Please hold." I did for about a minute then she was back. "I don't see a record for anyone by that name, but we only retain volunteer records for five years. When did Ms. Spencer work here?"

"Farther back than that, I'm afraid. Twelve years."

There was a pause. "That's pretty far back to go in someone's job history. Who did you say you work for?"

"I didn't. Suffice it to say, in our place of employment, it's absolutely essential not to leave a stone unturned." I knew she would infer that it was a security check for one of the federal intelligence agencies. It's exactly what I meant for her to infer. It was the logical place for her mind to go so close to DC. It was a crime for me to impersonate federal law enforcement, but there was nothing illegal about this woman drawing her own conclusions.

"I see," she said. "Well, our director has been here for fifteen years. Let me see if she can help you out. Hang on."

I waited another five minutes and had begun to wonder whether she'd forgotten me when a new voice came on the line.

"This is Kathy Burgess, the director here. I understand you're doing a...sensitive background check on a former volunteer."

"That's correct," I said, offering no further information. In these situations, it was always best to let the mark's imagination fill in the blanks. They were eager to imagine themselves as an ally to protecting national security.

"That's a long time ago, but I do remember Brooke Spencer. She had a particular knack with our residents. She was always going above and beyond to make them happy, working far more hours than her service club at school required. She organized a Senior Prom and made sure every resident had a young person to dance with. Every resident who went talked about that long after she left us to go to college. All of the ones she would have worked with have long since passed, but she was a ray of sunshine."

None of this surprised me. I would have been shocked to discover she *didn't* have an ease with the elderly. "Did she have any special connections with any of the residents in particular that you remember?"

"All of them, honestly. When she got into college, they pooled their resources and came up with a five-thousand dollar scholarship to help her pay for it."

The fine hairs rose on my neck, and alarm bells went off in my head. I'd expected to find that the trail started here, but this was a trailhead that began with a flashing neon sign. This was where Brooke Spencer must have learned that a little kindness toward the old could pay off literally.

"Did anything concern you about this transaction? Were you concerned about boundaries between her and your residents?"

"Oh no," the director said, almost rushing to reassure me. "In fact, she came to me, very worried about it because she said her parents could afford her tuition, and she didn't like our residents spending their money on her. But I told her to accept it with grace because it made them happy to feel like they were giving back. The fact that I can remember her so many years later despite all the volunteers who have come and gone should tell you that she was special."

I was unmoved by her praise of Brooke. The more someone's inner voice tried to whisper that something wasn't quite right about a person they trusted, the more they talked themselves into believing in that person's integrity. It was known as a "default to truth," a setting that allowed human society to thrive based on assumed honesty and trust. In reality, people who lied about important things were rare. That was a statistical fact. But the tiny fraction of deliberate liars who exploited that trust profited disproportionately.

Brooke may have even started at Landsdowne with the best of intentions but gotten a taste of what befriending old people could do for her. The temptation had proven too great, and Brooke's innate ability to win people's confidence had served her too well to allow her to walk away.

I thanked the director and hung up, moving on to my next "reference check," the think tank she'd worked for after college. It was well-known for its focus on public health, and as I researched it, I found multiple articles from politicians on both sides of the aisle quoting the think tank's findings in defense of their bills, amendments, and public health positions. Typical cherry-picking. The institute itself appeared reputable, but I had no luck getting in touch with anyone who had worked with Brooke directly. I was only able to get human resources to confirm that she had been employed there during the dates she listed and assure me that she had been marked as "eligible for re-hire."

That led me next to her job with her delegate to the Virginia General Assembly, a woman named Margaret Leeds, but I didn't bother trying to contact the assemblywoman. Even a state delegate wouldn't have time for a call like this, and chances were good she may not remember Brooke or have worked with her directly. This was a situation that called for the person who truly knew everything: the delegate's chief of staff.

"I'm sorry," the man said when he returned my phone call two hours later. "I've only been with the delegate for a year, after her former chief of staff retired, but I can give you her contact info. I'm sure Ellen would be happy to talk to you."

"That would be great," I told him, copying down the information. This was the part of private investigation work that got skipped over in TV and movies, the tedious chasing down of tiny details, the calls that sent you in circles, the emails sent that never got answers. But I was used to it, and it didn't bother me. I was a patient man when stalking my prey.

Especially when that prey was stalking Gran.

I emailed the former chief of staff immediately, but it was two days later before I got a response while I sat on a bench spying in the National Arboretum. It was a pretty park for sure, but a strange place for the vice president of a large credit agency to meet with one of K Street's most notorious lobbyists. I'd tailed the VP to the parking lot then did a quick clothing change in my car, switching into one of several outfits I kept on hand. My daily uniform was gray dress pants with a button down because I could easily throw on a sport coat and tie if I needed to blend in at the capitol or one of the popular power lunch spots in town, or I could remove the button up to reveal the T-shirt I wore advertising a 5K I'd never run if I needed to look more like a tourist.

I'd swapped out my pants for shorts and switched my office shoes for flip-flops, then grabbed my camera and headed into the arboretum a minute behind the VP, spotting her easily. I had settled onto my bench with my binoculars looking for all the world like a birdwatcher, when in reality I was watching them closely.

I didn't have any sound equipment, but I didn't need to. I needed only to establish a pattern of meetings between these two, so once I had a few closeup photos on my phone, I checked my email and found a reply from Ellen Brown.

Dear Mr. Norton,

I did indeed have the pleasure of supervising Brooke Spencer during her time with Delegate Leeds and would be happy to vouch for her.

Please call at your convenience.
Kind regards,
Ellen Brown

I pretended to follow another bird as it flitted in the opposite direction from my subjects, then exited the grounds when they were out of sight. I'd captured what I needed to for today.

I called Ellen Brown from the car, impatient to pick up Brooke's trail again. I was getting closer to the edge of the black hole in her resume. "Hello, this is Graham Norton calling for a reference check on Brooke Spencer," I said when a woman answered the call. I gave the name of the British talk show host I often used when I didn't want to advertise that I worked for Fleming, Roth, and Schill. No one ever recognized the name here. "Is this Ellen Brown?"

"It is. I'm happy to discuss Brooke with you. I have nothing but good things to say."

"Great. This should be a short call then. Let's start with the basics." I launched into a few questions for a standard reference check, and Brooke definitely sounded like a model employee.

"I find it interesting that her undergraduate degree was both in biology and political science," I noted. "That's an unusual pairing."

"Not really, not when you understand why," Ellen said, in her polite, professional voice. "She added political science late to her major after she took her semester of personal leave."

"Personal leave? Like a gap year?"

There was a pause. "Not like a gap year, no. But I don't think her reasons are relevant to an employment check."

Ah, here was another thread to follow, but I could sense that Ellen Brown was sharper than most. I would have to step carefully. "Back to her double major, what reason did she give for it?"

"Circumstances in her personal life prompted her to take on Big Tobacco, so—"

"Whoa, I'm sorry, did you just say she took on Big Tobacco? In

Virginia?" She said it like someone might say, "Brooke decided to go on a Sunday walk."

"Yes. I'm surprised this isn't in her resume." Ellen's voice had grown a degree cooler.

"She was being modest, I guess. Tell me about her advocacy work."

"She lobbied Delegate Leeds to introduce a bill to the General Assembly to ban the marketing of flavored vaping products to underage consumers. I think she thought studying political science would help, but she didn't need it. She was so effective that the delegate drafted the legislation based largely on Brooke's arguments and research, and it passed, making the Commonwealth the first state in the nation to explicitly outlaw some of the questionable marketing tactics of Big Tobacco. It was quite a feat given our state's long history with tobacco companies."

I had to concede that it was. "She sounds like an impressive young woman."

"I assume that's why you're considering her for a position with…"

"My company," I supplied, appreciative of her efforts to fish.

"Yes, your company. Well, as I said, she was a truly gifted young woman, and that's why we recruited her to our staff. It wasn't a surprise when Senator Rink's chief of staff lured her away, but it was a blow nonetheless."

There was no mention of Senator Rink's office in her LinkedIn profile. This was it. The missing piece. I pretended I knew this already. "So she went directly from your staff to his if I'm reading her resume correctly?"

"Correct."

Bingo. I'd found what should go in that employment gap. Why would Brooke choose to omit a prestigious job from her professional profile? The answer, I suspected, would unlock the whole mystery.

"Thank you for your time, Ms. Brown," I said. "You've been very helpful."

"Don't mention it. That's a young lady who deserves a fair shake."

We hung up with me pondering Ellen Brown's final words. "Deserves a fair shake," I mused aloud, using her same inflection.

Something in the way she said it implied she felt Brooke had *not* been treated fairly, and I'd bet my next paycheck that she was referring to the time in the senator's office that Brooke had tried to scrub from her history.

Unfortunately for Brooke Spencer, like the finest Virginia bloodhound, I had caught the scent of a trail, and I would chase down the truth. She would regret the day she'd ever crossed my path.

CHAPTER SIX

Brooke

The basket on my arm was heavy with more butternut squash as I slipped into my kitchen. I was finally coming to believe Miss Lily's assurances that her garden produced far more than even both of us plus Mary could eat.

"Why plant it all then?" I had asked that afternoon when Miss Lily plunked a third squash in my basket.

"I bring the extras over to the church. First Presbyterian. Lovely pastor. You should come with me."

"I might do that one of these Sundays."

"Anyway, we don't have a lot of great need in our congregation, but people sometimes get too busy for keeping a garden, and I love to bring them freshly picked vegetables to enjoy."

I smiled, remembering her answer. Miss Lily reminded me so much of the generous souls at Landsdowne when I'd volunteered there in high school. I was sure I'd gotten far more from the experience than the seniors I'd been assigned to befriend. Old people were my hands-down favorite, and Miss Lily was quickly becoming my very most favorite of all.

I settled in at my laptop to research butternut recipes, wondering if I was brave enough to try handmade pasta, when my phone vibrated with a call from my mom. I eyed it and considered sending her to voicemail. But she'd keep calling, leaving increasingly sad messages until I gave in and called back before I collapsed under the weight of all the daughter guilt. Best to get it over with.

I allowed myself a long, preemptive sigh before I answered. "Hey, Mom."

"Hey, honey. What are you doing?"

"I was out working in the garden."

"For that woman next door? Surely she can afford to hire someone."

I rolled my eyes. "Not *for* her, Mom. *With* her."

"But why? You complain about how busy preparing for the school year keeps you so that you can't come home, but then you spend all this time in the garden. Which is it?"

Linda Spencer did this often, simultaneously playing prosecutor like she had for five years out of law school before she stayed home to raise me, while also playing the role of neglected mother who needed her child to come dote on her and fill her empty nest.

In reality, she had an active social life, busy with home decorating, entertaining, and volunteer work. What she *actually* wanted was for me to abandon my job in sleepy Creekville and return home to McLean, take up the political career I'd left behind, and polish up the tarnish my stint in Senator Rink's office had left on the Spencer name.

I would absolutely not be doing that.

"The garden is giving me all kinds of ideas for lesson plans. And I might look into forming a club at the school where the kids put in a community garden on campus. We could even partner with the home ec class to have them cook things we grow. There are so many possibilities that I'm giddy just thinking about them."

This was met with a sniff, then silence as she marshalled her next argument.

I waited patiently, knowing there was no use trying to deflect it.

"Well, if you're already this busy, I can't even imagine how bad it will be when school starts. We won't see you until the holidays, and it's already been forever since you came to visit. You should come this weekend, before you're so overwhelmed that you can't get away."

"I was there a month ago," I reminded her. She had insisted we eat at the country club, nagged me into dressing up, then had conveniently run into a judge friend and his wife who had their son—an attorney my age—in tow. We'd ended up sitting together, me and the son who's name I'd already forgotten, soldiering on in polite conversation and trying to ignore the sidelong glances of our parents monitoring our progress.

"It seems so much longer," she complained. "And it'll be so long before you're here again. Come home this weekend."

"I can't, Mom. I have so much to do."

"The garden will be fine if you don't pick things for a couple of days."

"That's not true. It's important to pick things at their peak and no later. See all the things I'm learning already?"

"Is your life materially improved by knowing when you need to pick a tomato?" Her tone was growing ever-so-slightly sharp.

"Yes," I answered, my voice firm. It was the only way to deal with the Queen of Boundary-Crossing. "But garden aside, I have so much to do in my house."

"I still can't believe my uncle left you that old thing."

I realized my tactical error at once. I'd get a long lecture about how it was just like Fred to have saddled me with such an impractical inheritance and *why* didn't I simply sell it, and it would go on from there. For a while. A long, annoying while. I headed her off.

"I know. I can't believe how lucky I am. The bones of this place are so good. You'll be surprised when you see how much the right paint and some elbow grease can do."

"It's a poor use of your time," she complained. "There are people for that, same as there are to work in gardens. Hire someone else to do it and come home while your house gets painted. It'll be so much nicer than sitting in the noise and fumes."

It wouldn't be nicer. It would be full of more nagging, unsanctioned setups, and pressure to leave Creekville behind.

But it wouldn't get her anywhere. As a young woman, I hadn't seen through the life my parents lived. Not that either of my parents were bad people. They weren't. But my mom was so caught up in staying in the social mix that she'd lost herself. Or maybe she'd become nothing more than a reflection of the people she spent all her time around.

In hindsight, I could see how everything from the neighborhood where we'd lived to the volunteer activities my mother urged me toward had all been part of a carefully planned campaign to secure her place in the McLean social hierarchy. I hadn't thought much about being friends with the children of some of the nation's most important political figures. Like, it just seemed normal. I'd eaten meals in the homes of senators, had sleepovers with the kids of generals, worked on science projects and campaign posters for class offices at the dining tables of congresspeople.

Only after my disastrous time in Senator Rink's office did I look at it all differently. How many of my friends' parents had been liars, cheats, and predators, putting on a politically perfect face for the world while privately engaging in the most heinous conduct? I was sure there was more than one of my parents' friends who counted on their power to not only protect them but to keep enabling behavior they wanted kept in the dark.

All I knew was that the further I got from DC, the less I trusted the people who craved its air, and that meant I wasn't going back to McLean a second before obligation required of me.

Was thirty too old to be this cynical?

"So you'll hire painters and come home?" my mom prompted.

"No, I'm definitely staying here," I replied. "Think of this as a win for your parenting. You taught me to work hard with my mind, and now I'm learning to work hard with my body. That work ethic is a credit to you. Good job, Mom."

She made a sound that I would have taken as a snort if Linda Spencer were prone to such an inelegant noise, which she most definitely wasn't. "I just don't understand why you want to spend all your time in that dusty, smelly old lumber pile."

"Let me let you go," I said. There was no point in explaining it all again. "I need to get dinner ready and go make more dust."

"But Brooke—"

"Bye, Mom. Love you!"

I ended the call and decided that I'd lost the energy to tackle pasta from scratch. Calls with my mom had that effect on me. I wished I could make her understand how McLean felt like a trap after experiencing the simplicity of Creekville. But how did I politely say, "I wouldn't trade the smell of paint and sawdust for the reek of capital corruption for all the eligible bachelors in the world"?

One did not say such things, politely or otherwise. One simply took one's money and ran away from it as fast and as far as possible without looking back, no matter how much one's mother begged.

CHAPTER SEVEN

Ian

I paused my playlist and my run through Rock Creek Park to take an incoming call.

"Ian Greene." I kept each syllable crisp.

"Mr. Greene, this is Warren Holt at Senator Rink's office."

A wave of satisfaction rippled over me. This was the final layer to pull back and figure out what Brooke was hiding.

"Mr. Holt, thanks for returning my call." I'd called the senator's office for a reference check on Brooke, expecting to hear back from one of the senator's underlings, not his chief of staff. This was an interesting development. "We're very impressed with Brooke Spencer but we'd love to hear about your experience with her."

There was a long pause. "I'm surprised she listed her employment here on her resume."

I would have to play the next part carefully. "It's a prestigious job, so it makes sense to me, but it sounds like you may have concerns about her time there?"

Another pause. "She's without doubt a capable person. But sometimes, it takes more than that to be a good fit."

"Her work wasn't to your standard?"

"I'm sure you know that federal guidelines prevent me from doing more than confirming her dates of employment and position."

"Not if she listed you as a personal reference."

"I am certain she did not." His tone was cool to the point of icy.

"You're right. So you're saying you wouldn't rehire her."

"I would not rehire her."

I considered how to get more information. He clearly wanted to talk, or he would have delegated this call. "If Miss Spencer were to be hired for a position dealing with sensitive materials, and I were speaking to someone who thought she shouldn't be, but that person isn't at liberty to disclose more, how would you advise that I proceed?"

Warren Holt cleared his throat. "I couldn't say. Who knows where the truth might turn up? Even the gossip blogs get it right now and again."

"I understand. Thank you for your call, Mr. Holt. It's appreciated."

I hung up and smiled. Warren Holt had given me the next key, and I would use it immediately. I dialed a number I used when I needed to dig deep on someone.

It rang twice before a mellow voice answered. "This is Brandon."

"It's Ian Greene. How's my favorite bartender?"

"Hungry," Brandon answered.

"Then let me take you out for the juiciest steak in town."

"Today?"

"Yeah, lunch."

"Meet you there at noon."

I jogged the rest of my route, mind racing. Warren Holt clearly wanted me to know there was a problem with Brooke. And his implication was that it was something I'd find in the capital gossip machine, not Brooke's employment records.

Gossip meant...an affair, probably. That's what it always seemed to mean with attractive young women.

And no one knew more about political gossip than Brandon, the bartender who ran a blog called "Spilled Tea" under the alias Earl Grey. I was one of the only people who knew it was Brandon behind the blog, but it made perfect sense. Brandon worked for one of the most expensive caterers in the city. His laidback vibe made it possible for him to sidle up to house staff at residences all over the DC area. His MO was pouring free drinks for the client's personal staff after events and asking questions until he found someone who talked. Then he loosened them up with even more liquor. He got truths that would make their employers' hair curl if they knew how easily Brandon sweet-talked their staff.

"Spilled Tea" didn't care about the politics of the moment, but Brandon was very interested in the politicians—especially their indiscretions. If Brooke Spencer had ever featured in capital gossip, Brandon would know.

At noon, I spotted Brandon waiting for me outside of Hal's, the priciest steakhouse in the District.

"Let's eat," Brandon said as I walked up.

"And then we'll talk," I said.

Brandon smiled. "You know this lunch is going to cost you more than a ribeye, right?"

"It always does," I said. "And it's always worth it."

When we were settled and our orders had been taken, Brandon eyed me over the rim of his glass as he took a drink of his beer. "Well?" he asked, setting down the drink.

"Brooke Spencer."

Brandon narrowed his eyes like he was thinking, then shook his head. "Don't recognize the name."

"Former policy advisor to Senator Rink. Left his office somewhere eighteen months to two years ago."

The lines in Brandon's forehead smoothed out. "Ah."

"Ah?"

"Ah."

I shook my head. "What do you need besides the best ribeye in the city?"

"You know what I like about you? Your clients have some of the deepest pockets around. If this Brooke Spencer is who I think she is, the info should be worth an easy thousand."

I reached for my wallet. I'd come prepared. "The client is me. But I'm trying to protect my grandmother, so yes, a thousand is worth it."

But when I peeled off ten hundred-dollar bills, Brandon waved it off. "I like grandmothers. I'll spill for a single Franklin. I'll drink on you tonight and call it good. That, plus you'll finally have to tell me how you figured out I'm behind 'Spilled Tea.'"

"Not going to happen," I said. "Can't reveal my investigator secrets. But I'll give you two Franklins to ease the pain."

Brandon laughed and accepted the bills, tucking them into his shirt pocket. "One day I'll get it out of you."

He wouldn't, but Brandon would be disappointed if he ever did figure it out. It had been total luck. Brandon had tended bar at the firm's holiday party two years before, and while waiting for my whiskey, I'd been idly eavesdropping on Brandon's conversation with the junior associate in front of him. Brandon had said, "That's some high-class baloney" to describe a load of bull the associate was feeding him. A week later, the same phrase had appeared in "Spilled Tea." I hadn't heard anyone else use the phrase before or since. It hadn't taken me long to realize that Brandon held an ideal job for collecting secrets.

"So Brooke Spencer," I prompted.

"About a year ago, I was tending bar at a fundraising gala when Rink's chief of staff sits himself down and starts tossing back vodka. One of his staffers came over, and I think was trying to suck up to him, telling him, 'Oh, don't worry, Rink can afford it. She'll take the settlement and walk.' So I got curious, naturally." He paused to take another drink.

He couldn't have been half as curious then as I was now, but I waited. Brandon liked the pleasure of spinning out his story.

"Anytime there's talk of settlements, there's always something juicy involved. So when the chief of staff leaves because he doesn't like the suck-up, I start chatting up the staffer. 'Boss seems like he's in a bad mood,' that kind of thing. I tell him it sounds like some court thing went wrong, and he just snorts. 'More like went right if you're a money-hungry—" Brandon coughs and takes a sip. "Anyway, I got the sense that a mistress got paid off, when all was said and done."

I felt something inside that I shouldn't have, not after eight years of wading into these kinds of investigations: disappointment. I'd thought my low opinion of humanity in general couldn't get any lower. Apparently, I still had some capacity to be surprised. Brooke Spencer, the wholesome girl-next-door with her braids and freckles and baskets of squash, had carried on an affair with an old, married senator. And then she'd blackmailed him into silence.

It made me angry that it surprised me, but I kept my expression neutral, waiting to see if Brandon had any further info. "Did you have any sense of who the mistress was? Or if this was a recurring thing with Rink?"

Brandon shook his head. "I think Rink was a player twenty years ago when he first got to DC, but word was he'd straightened up and learned to fly right because his wife had threatened to clean him out financially if he embarrassed her with any more affairs. I think he's been pretty straight for the last decade or so. As for who the mistress was?" He tapped his glass against the tabletop, like he was distracted, thinking. "I could never confirm it, but about a week later, I was bartending at another event and I saw the same staffer. I got a few shots into him, and he grumbled about how their policy advisor just quit and now everyone had so much more work and he was tired of picking up the slack."

"Who was the policy advisor?"

"I Googled. Someone named...Brooklyn? I don't remember. But maybe it's this Brooke Spencer you're asking about. Her photo was on the senator's website. Young. Pretty. Exactly what I would expect. Two weeks later, it was gone. Some middle-aged guy had the job."

"Did you ever run the story?" I would have to dig through the Spilled Tea archives to see if I could read between the lines.

Brandon nodded. "I did, as a blind item. There wasn't enough proof to shout it from the rooftops." He took another sip of his drink and watched me closely. "Why are you interested? You looking for dirt on Rink?"

"No," I answered. "Just have concerns about something my gran is getting mixed up in." A conversation with Brandon was always a negotiation. His currency was gossip, and so long as he saw me as a valuable source for it, he'd keep sharing his own for the price of a trade, plus some cash. Since I'd already given him $200, it was time to pay up with gossip of my own.

"I have something you may want to sniff out. An affair, and the worst sort of cliché: it's the pool boy."

Brandon smiled. "Spill."

"I'll let you figure out the details, but I'd say the Speaker needs to keep an eye on what's happening in his own house."

"Wait, house or *the* House?" Brandon asked.

I shrugged. "Does the House of Representatives have a pool I don't know about?" I didn't mind giving up the Speaker one bit. It might be his wife cheating this time, but I had no doubt he wasn't any more faithful. He was just marginally more discreet.

"That is very good tea," Brandon said, already pulling out his phone. "Going to send out some feelers unless you want to give up the details now?"

"I do not," I said, smiling. I'd given him a story that would break one way or the other within the next week. The client who had hired us to spy on the Speaker's business would make sure of it. The client wanted to bog the Speaker down right when he needed all of his attention on blocking a major bill the president wanted passed.

It was almost enough to make me roll my eyes. If the American people knew how much got done by blackmail rather than statesmanship, it would shred any lingering faith they had in their leaders.

"Well, this has been a surprisingly tasty lunch already and the steak isn't even here," Brandon said.

"Good. Now, tell me something I don't know about capital shenanigans."

We settled into a comfortable chat with Brandon sharing breezy gossip from the socialite circuit. I didn't find these kinds of stories interesting, but I always filed them away. I never knew when they would be helpful down the road for a case. It happened often enough for me to never dismiss the power of idle chatter to solve major cases when I least expected it.

Still, the whole time I listened to Brandon, my mind ran down a separate track, planning my next weekend visit to Gran. I needed a gentle way to break it to her that her new friend was one of the most devious liars I'd ever investigated.

I didn't love the idea of disillusioning Gran, but I did look forward to the expression on Brooke's face when I exposed her as a con artist. It was the very best part of my day job, but no victory there would ever be more satisfying than rooting Brooke out of Gran's life.

CHAPTER EIGHT

Brooke

I shielded my eyes against the late afternoon sun and sighed.

"Don't worry," Miss Lily said. "Plenty of time until sunset. This won't take us too much longer." She pulled another weed and moved to the next tomato plant as if to prove her point.

"It's not that."

"Then what?"

I hesitated then pasted on a smile. "Nothing."

"Not nothing. Something. You seem off today. Tell me what's going on."

I looked over the garden and tried to draw some comfort from its bright colors and orderly rows.

"Come on, honey. Spit it out. You'll feel better," Miss Lily urged.

I took a deep breath. "It's just that my anxiety likes to creep up on me sometimes, and it doesn't always make sense. Race you down the row." I pulled out the next few weeds with extra hard yanks, but still, the anxiety clung to me like dirt to the roots.

It was silly, but since her obnoxious grandson had pulled up at this same time last week, I worried he'd make a repeat appearance to antagonize me again.

You're being ridiculous. This happened every time I got stressed, and now with only two weeks until my very first day as a high school teacher, I was highly stressed. Like Washington Monument high. And that aggravated my anxiety. And my anxiety led to catastrophizing.

Stop it.

I worked through one of the exercises from my therapist, breathing in for several slow counts, holding it, then breathing out again. *Be present. Enjoy the sun and soil.*

I'd just managed to calm down when the sound of a car door slamming echoed through the peaceful afternoon birdsong like a gunshot. I squeezed my eyes shut and took a deep breath. Maybe it wasn't him?

But no. A minute later, Ian was rounding the house toward the garden. I dropped my eyes down to my weeding. Miss Lily hadn't noticed him yet, and I had a few moments to school my expression into something polite. I could pretend he wasn't the last person I wanted to see. I could think of at least two other people I'd rather see less. If I tried. Probably?

"Gran!" he called.

And when Miss Lily's head turned in Ian's direction, her face beaming, I clenched my jaw and forced another smile.

"Ian!" Miss Lily cried, hopping to her feet with the energy and grace that never failed to amaze me. She rushed toward him and stepped into his hug.

I really, really did not like that man. How could someone as awesome as Miss Lily produce a grandson as stuck-up and judgy as Ian?

I hoped I'd managed to control my expression when Miss Lily waved me over with an order to, "Come say hello!"

What was it about this man that tied my stomach in knots?

It wasn't like he made me nervous in a good way. He made me nervous in a bad way. In a Harrison Rink and Warren Holt kind of way.

Since I'd been a teenager, if I couldn't navigate a situation with humor, I'd been able to navigate it with grit.

Until them.

Until Rink.

Until he'd stripped my sense of self away and left me clawing for any semblance of security.

That was over. I'd found my last bit of courage and left, but I'd lost so much of myself in the process. And now, a big, arrogant, entitled jerk like Ian was all it took to make me feel small again.

I rose from the dirt and squared my shoulders. No more. I was done making myself small for anyone.

"Hello, Ian." I crossed the garden to join Miss Lily. "We don't see you for months and now you're here for two weekends in a row. How…nice."

He blinked, his eyes narrowing for the tiniest second before he recovered. Good. He didn't miss my real meaning. "I forgot until last weekend how much I like being out here. I won't make the mistake of leaving Gran alone so often again."

Why did that sound like a warning? What was this guy's problem?

"I'm hardly alone, Ian," Miss Lily objected as she slid her arm through his. "Mary is always great company, and Brooke here has been an absolute breath of fresh air."

"I agree with Ian," I said. "There's no real substitute for family, is there?" *Come around more, you selfish idiot. Heaven knows why your grandmother ever misses you, but she does.*

"Can't argue with that," Ian said. "And I'm here to make sure you get all the love and attention you need." He dropped a kiss on his gran's fluffy white hair.

"I always have that in spades, but I'll never say no to more." She smiled up at him.

"Well, I'll leave you two to enjoy each other," I said. "I need to get dinner started anyway."

"I'm glad you're here, actually," Ian said. "I was pretty distracted last weekend and I didn't have a chance to get to know you very well.

I'd love to get to know Gran's first new neighbor in years and thank you for keeping an eye on my favorite person."

"That's an excellent idea, Ian. Such a good boy. You should take her out to dinner."

"That's not what I meant, Gran."

"Doesn't mean it's not a good idea," Gran said. "You should go to Caps! As in mushrooms," she added, smiling at me.

"Uh, sorry?" Had I missed a step in the conversation?

"Caps specializes in mushroom dishes. Funny name for a restaurant, isn't it? Don't worry, they make plenty of other delicious dishes too. Best risotto I've had outside of Florence. Get that."

Yeah, right. The last thing I wanted to do was spend an awkward evening trying to dodge Ian's jabs. I opened my mouth to say so, but Miss Lily spoke up first.

"You'll love it. They do a peach shortbread with a whipped mascarpone topping that is to die for. And at eighty, I don't say that lightly."

"Oh, I don't think tonight will work," I said. "I've got so much work to do still."

"You just said you were going to make dinner. Use that time to let someone else make it for you, and Ian is an added bonus. He's a charming dinner companion."

I had never had a reason to doubt Miss Lily until now. Clearly, she had some bias here. Ian had been anything but charming up to this point. I tried to sidestep the invitation again. "That's all right. You two should go enjoy it. You can tell me all about it tomorrow."

"Nonsense," Miss Lily declared. "I can't get a moment's peace when I go into town to eat. Everyone wants to stop by my table and visit. But you two will be left alone, and it will make me happy to sit and have a peaceful night with Mary and imagine you two enjoying some truly divine cooking."

There was no way to escape this gracefully. I couldn't care less about offending Ian, but offend Miss Lily? I'd rather eat wormy dirt.

"Gran's never wrong about food," Ian said. "What do you say we give it a try? I'll swing by at seven-thirty."

"Sure." I offered my most neighborly smile, but the slight twitch on

Ian's lips suggested I must look more annoyed than neighborly. Too bad. "But I want to be home early, so make it seven o'clock." The sooner we started, the sooner we'd get it over with.

"Sounds great. I'll be there promptly."

"Good boy," Miss Lily said, patting his arm. "Now you come help me finish this weeding so Brooke can go gussy up."

"I'm not going to gussy up," I protested.

"Definitely don't bother on my account," Ian said. "Creekville won't mind your understated look."

My "understated look"?! Oh, I'd show him "understated." But all I said was, "See you soon." Then I gathered my garden tote and headed toward my house without a backward glance.

When a knock sounded on the door at exactly seven o'clock, I glanced over my reflection and gave the sexy woman smiling back at me a wink. I'd taken a long shower to steam the garden dirt from beneath my nails and off my skin. I'd worked with the humidity and applied some curl spray while I dried my hair, leaving the long strands to fall in loose waves that looked more dark gold than light brown tonight. I couldn't do much about covering my freckles, but I didn't care. I liked the feel of the sun streaming down on my head and shoulders while I worked in the garden without a hat, and the freckles were a fair trade.

I'd picked a sleeveless coral shift and four-inch sandals, determined to limit the amount of looming Ian Greene could do with the six inches of height he had on me. I topped it off with a pearl pendant on a thin silver chain. "You got class for days, sis." *Understated*, Ian had said. I snorted. Understated *elegance*, maybe. What a jagweed.

I went to answer the door before he could knock again. I pulled it open just as he lifted his hand. The result was him standing with his fist in the air, pointlessly, while he looked confused at having nothing to do with it. *Maybe punch your own face, dude*. But he just let it drift down after a second.

"You look nice."

Nice? I lifted an eyebrow. "Don't sound so surprised."

"Uh, right." He gave me a quick scan, and I appreciated that it didn't feel creepy. "Well, I guess we should go?" He stepped back to let me pass.

I smiled once I was sure he couldn't see me because I knew I would only look smug. He'd clearly expected to find me in overalls and Miss Lily's garden dirt, "understated" for dinner. But I was Linda Spencer's daughter, raised in the cotillions and country clubs of one of the wealthiest zip codes in the country, and I definitely knew how to clean up "nice." Poor dummy.

My smugness lasted exactly three seconds until my heel caught on a nail in the porch board I'd been meaning to hammer down for a month. I pitched forward, windmilling toward the stairs. I squeaked and swung my arms in a wild effort to regain my balance, but I tilted, tilted, tilted—

And suddenly found myself upright again, yanked back by Ian's strong arm wrapped around my waist, holding me against his chest.

His hard, broad chest.

"You okay?" His voice was a warm rumble against my back.

"Fine." Had that been a hint of laughter in his voice? "Been meaning to take care of that nail for a while."

"Nail?"

"Yes." I pushed lightly at his arm and took the three steps leading to the front path. I turned and pointed to the offending nail. "I tripped on that."

"Sure. High heels must be tricky if you're not used to them, especially when you have random nails trying to sabotage you."

Not used to them? Like I was a ten-year-old playing dress up? And was his voice a touch *too* understanding when he said that? Oh, he was smooth. I'd have to stay sharp to keep up with all his passive-aggressive insults. He was good enough for me to wonder if my mother had raised him too.

Ugh. The last thing I wanted to do was spend the evening navigating subtext with a guy I couldn't stand, but at least I had the skills for it. *Do your worst, Ian Greene. I'm ready.*

The drive to Caps was short, only ten minutes, filled with sporadic small talk about the weather and Miss Lily's garden.

We took the last spot in the parking lot. It was a good sign that the restaurant was bustling. A quiet restaurant parking lot on a Friday night wouldn't suggest good food, but Caps was hopping. Now I had to hope that we weren't stuck with a long wait, making more awkward small talk.

"Table for two," Ian said to the smartly dressed hostess when we stepped into the crowded entry.

I tried not to stress. Great. Long wait and awkward chatter it would be.

"Name, please?" the hostess asked.

"Ian."

"Greene?" She asked, looking up from her list.

"Yes," he confirmed with a note of surprise.

"Your table is ready. Miss Lily called ahead."

Ian smiled. "Of course she did."

"She also said to tell you not to be mad, but she ordered for you."

This earned her a laugh from Ian, and I had to smile too.

"Also not a surprise," he said. "Can't wait to find out what I'm having for dinner."

The hostess led us to a cozy booth tucked into the back corner of the restaurant, far from the bustle of kitchen traffic. She left us with a smile and not a single menu.

"Gran is a tiny tyrant," Ian said.

"A benevolent tyrant." I wrinkled my nose in a way an ex-boyfriend had called adorable, so I'd broken up with him. Kittens were adorable. Not grown women. "Is that a thing? A benevolent tyrant?"

"It's a pretty accurate description," Ian said. "So I guess it's a thing."

A waiter approached the table with a bottle of wine. "A Chenin blanc, courtesy of Mrs. Greene," he said, pouring a generous glass for each of us. "Oaked, with buttery top notes."

"A dry white," Ian said. "Interesting. I'm guessing we're having poultry."

The first course was the stuffed mushroom caps Miss Lily had raved over. I bit into one and gave a nod. "She wasn't lying. These are delicious. I have faith in whatever else she chose."

"Gran has excellent taste. Usually."

There it was again, that hint of … something in his voice. An undercurrent. I wasn't imagining it.

What was the best way to disarm this man so that he'd stop with his overbearing protectiveness of his grandmother? Miss Lily could handle herself with anyone, and I posed no threat to her. She'd vaulted over a dozen people in line ahead of her to become my favorite in a month flat.

Maybe this called for a charm offensive. I could pull out my best, most sparkly cocktail party self, brush off a few anecdotes, convince him of my friendliness, and then maybe he wouldn't feel the need to supervise me at every turn. Because it definitely felt like Ian the Investigator from the bigshot DC firm had me squarely in his sights.

I stifled a sigh. That type of suspicion was bad for the soul, especially if it led him to suspect someone as unobjectionable as me of… anything, honestly. But that was par for the course with people who spent too much time in DC. I hadn't escaped without acquiring my own shell of cynicism.

The world needed less of that. And maybe mustering up some charm to get Ian Greene to back down was its own kind of cynicism, but it was the right move. If he'd truly rediscovered a love of visiting his grandma, well…I could admire that. Maybe I could keep that in mind if he was going to be a regular weekend nuisance.

Visitor. Time to give him the benefit of the doubt. Weekend *visitor.*

"Miss Lily seems happy to have you here two weeks in a row. It's sweet of you to come out."

"There's nothing I wouldn't do for her."

Again, his tone held a note of warning. I dabbed at my mouth with the thick linen napkin and tried to find one last bit of goodwill toward this obnoxious man.

Nope. I had nothing.

"You have a tone." I cut right to the heart of my annoyance.

"Tone? What do you mean?"

I rolled my eyes. "You talk like you're the smartest guy in the room, holding onto secrets no one else knows. It reads as smug. You did it just now, with your fake innocent, 'What do you mean?' And comments like how Miss Lily has excellent taste except when it comes to me somehow." I set the napkin on the table and leaned toward him. "Say what you want to say, Ian. I'm tired of subtext."

His expression didn't give away much. He watched me for a long, measured moment before he nodded. "All right. I know what you're up to with my grandmother. And I'm watching. Back off."

My mouth dropped slightly, but I literally had no words.

"Don't play dumb," he said, his voice growing rough. "My investigation of you over the last week has shown that you may be a scammer, but you're definitely not stupid."

"Your 'investigation'? What exactly do you think I'm up to with Miss Lily? Trying to wheedle all of her best gardening tips out of her? Guilty. I scammed her out of her secret fertilizer for tomatoes: coffee grounds. You got me."

"Don't be cute," he said. "I promise you I'm taking this very seriously. You may have fooled your uncle, but Gran has *me* watching out for her."

I wasn't sure if I was more confused or indignant. Both emotions were fighting for the upper hand.

Confused, I decided. "I have no idea what you're talking about. It's nice that you've shown up after months to express some interest in your grandmother's life, but what does that have to do with my uncle?" I wasn't playing stupid, I *felt* stupid, like I was trying to play catch up, and I hated feeling stupid.

"You forget what I do for a living. I never take people at their word because I have too much evidence that I shouldn't. So I've been digging into you over the last week, uncovering your tracks."

His words sent a physical pang through my stomach, a wave of queasiness even though I'd eaten nothing but a mushroom cap with a sip of wine. If he was talking about the senator ...

"I'll paint a picture." He set his wineglass down hard enough to slosh it. "You volunteer in a nursing home in high school and con those lonely old people into funding a scholarship that they can't afford, and it gives you a taste for what's possible. I'm not sure what other scams you pulled, but the next one that shows up is you going to visit your uncle with whom you had little prior relationship, and suddenly he's leaving everything to you in his will. And somehow in the middle of all that, you manage to have an affair with a married senator that results in a big financial settlement for you that I can only assume is to buy your silence. It certainly explains why Highmark Wealth Management would take you on as a client when nothing in your job or family history would point to that kind of income." He patted his own mouth with his napkin and set it down with studied indifference. "How did I do?"

How did he do? *How did he DO?*

My fists clenched as I resisted the bodily urge to reach across the table and wipe the smirk off his face. I took three slow breaths in, then out, and finally uncurled my hands to reach for my phone.

I opened the rideshare app and requested a car. Creekville didn't have much of a Lyft force, but it also meant the few drivers were always available. *Five minutes.* I could handle five minutes if four of them were spent outside on the sidewalk, away from Ian's smug face.

"Nothing to say for yourself?" he asked.

"Not really." I slid my chair back. "Seems you know everything you need to." I rose and slung the thin strap of my purse over my shoulder. I took a step for the door but paused beside him. "Then again, maybe it would interest you to know that I donated that scholarship to Alzheimer's research, and that Fred left his house to his seven nieces and nephews and I bought them all out at market value."

His forehead furrowed. I didn't know if it was confusion or doubt, but I didn't care. "Your investigation missed another important detail: I'm a woman of action over words." I snatched up his mostly full glass of wine and tossed it in his face before walking out of the restaurant.

My timing was perfect, for once. I hit the sidewalk as the blue Nissan assigned to me pulled up to the curb. I confirmed with the woman behind the wheel that she was there for me, then opened the back door to slide in.

"Brooke," Ian called as I reached to pull the door closed.

I turned to see him standing on the sidewalk, a wet spot staining the front of his light gray button-down shirt.

"What about the senator?" he asked.

I thought about flipping him off but refrained. Barely. "NDA," I called and slammed the door shut. "Go ahead," I told the driver.

I waited until the restaurant was firmly in the rearview mirror before I cried.

CHAPTER NINE

Ian

I walked back into the restaurant. The other diners stared as I made my way to the booth in the corner. I didn't know if they'd seen Brooke toss the wine. More likely it was me running out after her that had drawn their notice. Either way, I ignored them all as I sat down to think.

NDA. A non-disclosure agreement. It could still be the senator's effort to keep her quiet about an affair. But if she was telling the truth about her donation and the house, then that made me second guess the affair.

Had I been wrong?

I went over the evidence in my mind. Her narrative could fit all of it except for one gaping hole: Gran's wanting to leave her home to Brooke. That had all the markings of a skilled scammer, and skilled scammers always had innocent explanations for their windfalls.

I studied the tablecloth without seeing anything. The waiter approached with two plates and a look of complete confusion.

"Sir, will your friend be rejoining you?"

Friend. Ha. "No, just box those up." I'd bring them home to Gran.

"Very good."

The waiter slipped away as quietly as he had come. He could have escorted himself off with a brass band and I still might not have paid him any attention. I was too distracted trying to parse Brooke's words, picking them apart to find the truth.

Well, I wasn't going to find it here in Caps. When the waiter returned with a fancy bag, our dinners packaged inside, I accepted it and left with a word of thanks and a large tip. The guy deserved hazard pay after surviving the drama we'd served up.

I needed to think before going back to Gran's. I took one of the country roads leading out of Creekville, the car quiet, my mind racing faster than the wheels. It all came back to the same thing: I could believe Brooke if Gran weren't changing her will. But that was irrefutable proof that Brooke was a schemer.

It made sense, really. The fresh-faced gardener didn't fit the profile for someone who would pull off the kind of scams I'd uncovered. But the sophisticated woman I'd picked up for dinner was a different story. She'd answered the door looking so beautiful and polished that it had startled me into silence. Cute had become sexy. But her warmth had also turned chilly. The woman who had answered the door was one I could easily imagine seducing a senator and walking away with a payoff.

I'd have to dig deeper to uncover proof beyond the circumstantial evidence.

Good thing that was my specialty.

I turned the car toward Gran's, and by the time I pulled into her driveway, the porch light burned, but the rest of the house was dark. I'd have to talk to her in the morning and break her heart with the truth about Brooke, but I'd do it a hundred times if it kept Gran safe.

"Ian Davis Greene, you come down here right now."

I swam up from sleep to the sound of Gran's voice calling from the bottom of the stairs. Even with my door shut, I could hear her clearly.

"*Now*," she repeated, and thirty-three years old or not, I knew better than to make her say it one more time.

I grabbed the UVA shirt from the chair beside me and pulled it on even as I stumbled out to face angry Gran. "Good morning, Gran."

"It most certainly is not," she snapped. "What did you do to my poor Brooke?"

I reached the bottom of the stairs and blinked down at her, still fuzzy from sleep. I hadn't yet marshalled the arguments I'd meant to make to Gran about why Brooke was bad news. "Can I get some coffee before we do this?"

"No. You may not."

I nodded and sank down on the bottom step so I wasn't towering over her.

"She was supposed to meet me in the garden this morning, but she wasn't there." Gran glared at me. "That's very unlike her, Ian. Very. So after fifteen minutes I popped over to check on her. She says she won't set foot in the garden until you go back to DC."

"Probably for the best."

"Proba—" She broke off and glared at me, her hands going to her hips. Uh-oh. "What is wrong with you, child? Brooke Spencer is constant sunshine and now she's afraid to come play in my garden because of you. I repeat: what did you do?"

"I know you like her, Gran, but she's not who she says she is."

Gran's eyes narrowed. "That young woman living next door isn't Brooke Spencer?"

"No, I mean, that's her name, but she's not the innocent, helpful neighbor she pretends to be."

"Are you trying to tell me I'm a bad judge of character?"

"I have proof."

"This I have to hear." Gran didn't look like she was predisposed to believe a word that came out of my mouth.

"Coffee."

"Come on."

I trailed her into the kitchen but waved her into a chair when she headed for the coffee pot. "I've got it, Gran." I poured hers just like she liked it, two sugars and a healthy dollop of cream. "I've been looking into Brooke this week."

"Why?"

"Because I think she's taking advantage of you."

"That's insulting to my intelligence and judgment. I think the only time I have ever been wrong about a person's character in my life is right this second, where I'm calling into question whether you have the common sense God gave a goat."

"She puts up a good front. I think it's why she's been so effective in fleecing her string of victims without ever drawing the notice of the authorities."

"A 'string of victims'? Maybe you better lay out that evidence." Spoken like a law dean's wife.

I started with the way the nursing home residents had given her five thousand dollars then moved to the strange gaps in her resume, her departure from Senator Rink's office with a financial settlement that reeked of hush money, and ended with the inheritance of her distant uncle's estate.

"Estate," Gran repeated with a snort. "Hardly. He left her a house with good bones that he didn't update once in forty years. Headache is more like it. But that girl has grit, and she'll polish it to a shine yet."

I couldn't believe it. I'd laid out compelling evidence and she was still singing Brooke's praises. This was worse than I thought.

I clenched my jaw. No matter. I'd get through to Gran because I had to. And if it meant calling in reinforcements, I'd do that too, but I really hoped I'd be able to find a way to make Gran see reason.

"Gran, doesn't any of that smell at all fishy to you?"

"The only thing that stinks around here is your judgment," she said. "You are dead wrong about that girl."

"But—" I broke off as my phone buzzed in my pocket. I fumbled it out to silence it but then I saw the number. "I'm sorry, Gran, I need to take this."

"Ian Davis Greene, you better not—"

"I'll be quick. I promise. Hello?" I said as I stepped onto Gran's back patio.

KISS ME NOW

"Is this Graham Norton? Or perhaps I should say Ian Greene?"

I remembered Ellen Brown's voice well. Brooke's former boss had sounded cool when I last spoke to her, but now she sounded downright frosty.

"This is Ian." I kept my voice neutral, waiting to see what had prompted her call.

"I received a most concerning call from Brooke Spencer last night," she said. "It seems you aren't at all who you pretended to be when we last spoke."

"With all due respect, neither is Brooke."

"If Brooke is behaving as a circumspect young woman with a maturity beyond her years and a kindness you rarely find in people anymore, then she's showing you exactly who she is."

"If you say so." I would bet very little got past Ellen Brown. How had she too been taken in?

"I do say so," Ellen Brown snapped, "and do not get glib with me. Brooke called me last night because one of her worst nightmares came true: her past caught up to her, but apparently not in the way you think. She will not thank me for making this phone call, but I'm not bound by the same non-disclosure agreement she is, and I won't stand for that morally bankrupt senator causing her more misery than he already has. Now you listen and you listen good."

"Yes, ma'am," I said, the first tickle of discomfort whispering through my chest. "I'm listening."

"You thought it was odd that Brooke majored in political science and biology. She only ever intended to major in biology, maybe go into research, but during her sophomore year, her roommate developed a serious lung infection from vaping and died. Brooke was heartbroken. She took a semester off school to grieve. But she's incredibly resilient, and when she went back, she was determined to make a difference. She added poly-sci to her major and began lobbying Delegate Leeds to sponsor the bill banning the sale of the flavored vape products that tobacco companies are using to hook young people. Her advocacy caught my eye, and I recruited her to our staff when she graduated."

The discomfort grew to something more like a prickle. "None of this is in her professional profile. Why wouldn't she include that?"

"Modesty, honestly," Ellen Brown said. "She felt it was a team effort, but it was her passion that was the impetus for all of it. But she was also deeply loyal to her roommate and doesn't like her name dragged up in connection with tragedy. Brooke doesn't feel people should be defined by them."

"Did you verify all of this?" I asked.

"You mean did I have that dead roommate's parents sit in my office and weep when they recounted the pain of the week their daughter spent dying? Yes."

Her voice was a slap, and I deserved it. "I'm sorry," I said quietly. "Continue."

"Brooke's work was tireless and impeccable. She drew a lot of notice for her passionate advocacy, and it wasn't very long before other offices began to sniff around, hoping to recruit her. She fielded interest from several commonwealth administrations, all the way up to the governor's office. But she's loyal, remember? It wasn't until Senator Rink's chief of staff requested that she come meet with them about passing federal vaping standards that she considered what impact she could have beyond Virginia. She'd seen that with the right people, change really can happen, and God forgive me, I encouraged her to pursue the opportunity with Rink." Her voice trembled a tiny bit.

Regret? Anger? I wasn't sure. "Why do you think you need forgiveness for that?"

"Because I sent a lamb to the slaughter. Brooke is genuinely *good*. I knew DC waters were sometimes murky, but I had no idea how truly deep the swamp could go. We'd talk a couple of times a month or get lunch sometimes. And the stories she told me about the way even her own colleagues would connive and backstab turned my stomach. I could literally feel my blood pressure rising. And that didn't even turn out to be the worst of it."

"The senator was." It was clear where this story was going.

"Yes," she confirmed. "I knew about his womanizer reputation. But the rumors were years in the past. And Brooke may be young, but at twenty-six, she wasn't naïve. She could handle herself. And she did," she said, a bitter note creeping into her voice. "But she couldn't handle the senator. I'm not sure anyone could. He's a skilled predator, and Brooke didn't see it coming until it was too late."

"What happened?" A complicated shift in my emotions was taking place, one I wasn't sure I could fully describe. My contempt for Brooke wasn't dissipating so much as it was transferring to the senator as Ellen's story unfolded.

"He groomed her. Brooke is about action, so pretty words have never done it for her. But when the senator began to hand her plum assignments on top of the compliments he regularly paid her work, she was thrilled. She felt like she was 'in the room where it happened,' as the saying goes. He began to defer to her opinions and include her in his inner circle of aides. It caused a lot of friction with the other staff, and it bothered her, but she pushed on, excited about getting a chance to work on her ideas on a bigger stage. And then the tone slowly began to change."

"Let me guess," I said. I'd sat through too many depositions not to know what came next. "The compliments went from professional to personal. The meetings went from small to just the two of them."

"Bingo," Ellen said. "One night when they were on a fact-finding trip in Chicago, he called her to his room to give her a copy of a report."

I winced, knowing what was coming next.

"He came onto her strong, but it wasn't Weinstein-level. She called me, shaken up, but decided it was because he was drunk, and they were on the verge of getting the bill co-sponsored, so she decided she would give him another chance. I told her she needed to resign immediately, that she would have no problem finding another job, but she said she wanted to wait until the bill made it to a vote and then she would quit.

"But a couple of weeks later, the chief of staff called her to the office one night, said they wanted to go over the senator's speech introducing the bill the next day. When she got there, it was only the senator. And he did not believe that she didn't want a chance to sleep with one of the most powerful men in the country."

"Did he…" I couldn't even force myself to ask the words.

"He tried," Ellen confirmed, voice grim. "Brooke left with a ripped skirt, some missing buttons, and some red marks. She called her mother in tears. Her mother made sure they had pictures of the physical marks. That was her lawyer training, I expect. But she also advised Brooke against going to the police. Said she'd only be dragged through every newspaper and TV broadcast as a trashy headline with no guarantee of justice."

I wished I could say that I didn't understand her mother's cynicism, but I did. Many good people worked in the criminal justice system, but it was a crapshoot to get a sexual assault conviction. Those odds grew far worse when someone as powerful as the senator was involved.

"Instead, her mother hired Jansen Davies."

I gave a low whistle. Jansen was the toothiest shark in East Coast private practice.

"Yes," Ellen confirmed. "And he made Rink pay. Dearly." She fell quiet, then added, "I'm ambivalent about the NDA. I think speaking out—even if some didn't believe her—would do a lot to warn women in the future that the senator's predation is ongoing."

"Yeah. I get that." I'd often had the same thought when our firm had tied up women in NDAs to protect the reputations of powerful men. Did it just enable more of the same? "It sounds like a sizable settlement."

"Over a million," Ellen confirmed. "Brooke never cared about the money, but she knew that no matter what she did, rumors about the settlement would make the rounds. She wanted to ensure that the amount was painful enough to force Rink to make sure he never preyed on anyone again for fear of future lawsuits. She's still angry that all this cost him only money, while her reputation took the shot. Some days, she feels like it only underlines her mother's wisdom in not pursuing a criminal case. Some days, I think she wishes she had burned it all to the ground, no matter what the consequences. But most days, I think she tries very hard to forget. And still, the rumors pop up that the gorgeous young aide seduced the senator."

I cleared my throat, knowing I was going to do something I had rarely had to do in my career. "I was wrong about Brooke."

"You were," Ellen confirmed. "Do you know what she did for the first several months after she quit? She went to stay with her uncle to pull herself together and to get off Rink's radar. Then she moved in with her mom and volunteered as a tutor every day in one of DC's underperforming high schools."

More and more pieces of the puzzle fell into place. "That turned her on to teaching."

"It did. Brooke is a woman who needs a purpose, and she felt like she made a real difference there. When she discovered she'd partially inherited her uncle's house around the time she completed her teaching credential, she took it as an opportunity to escape all of the lingering capital gossip."

"And then I showed up."

"And then you showed up."

I thought about Gran in the next room, ready to finish tearing me up over my misjudgment of Brooke. It was time to listen to the wisdom of these two women. "I'll apologize to her."

"I think if you just left her alone, that would be enough."

But I wasn't so sure I could. I really did owe her at least the apology. And Ellen Brown too, I realized. "I'm sorry about the false pretenses of the first call. I thought I was protecting my grandmother from a scammer, and there isn't much I wouldn't do for her."

"It's partially my fault," Ellen said. "I knew Brooke had a teaching job. I should have called and asked her about this supposed reference check myself, but she often comes to see me when she visits her parents, and I guess I figured we'd catch up then. And it's good you keep an eye on your grandmother."

"I'm not sure she thinks so right now," I said, and Ellen laughed at my tone. "She likes Brooke and I've scared her into hiding, so I'm in the doghouse."

"You definitely deserve it," Ellen answered. "But I suspect she won't stay mad at you for long."

I apologized again and thanked her for her time, then hung up, took a deep breath, and tried to figure out how I was going to face Gran.

CHAPTER TEN

Brooke

I straightened and stretched my back, glaring down at the kitchen floor with all the contempt I normally reserved for Brussel sprouts or spiders. Uncle Fred or his wife had laid down a faux-tile linoleum over the wood floors, and I'd been at work for two hours with a scraper trying to peel it up and chip the glue away. It had to be at least forty years old, but it clung like it was newly cemented, and my shoulders and back ached.

I'd much rather get these sore muscles from working in the garden with Miss Lily, but Ian had ruined that for me.

Ian. What a jerk.

The sickly feeling I got anytime I thought about Senator Rink or my time on his staff crept up on me. Prickly palms. Overwarm cheeks. A touch of nausea. I wished I could simply step outside and take in some fresh air, but I didn't want to risk it if it meant running into Ian.

I walked to the front of the house, rolling my shoulders and neck to rid them of tightness. It didn't help. I stopped at the large picture window and peered through the curtains. I could barely see the front fender of Ian's car, but the grill was distinctive. It was his.

I let the curtain fall, a frustrated sigh escaping me. What I needed more than anything was time in the garden. Not that I had the time to spare. Not with all the work left to do on the house, lesson planning, and classroom prep. But I'd learned to make time for it anyway because being in the garden had become an anchor for me, a therapy I needed. When I sat in the fresh soil, the sharp tang of growing plants tickling my nose, the hum of insects and birdsong in the background, the sun shining down…somehow all of that with the steady rhythm of the day's work—weeding or harvesting—signaled the most anxious parts of my brain to relax so good ideas could bubble up.

The same thing happened when I showered too. Something about the steady rhythm of the water and my wandering mind always led me to great ideas. It happened so often that I'd begun keeping a dry erase marker in the stall so I could write notes on the tile instead of having the ideas dry up by the time I got myself dry. The garden did the same thing.

I resented more than ever that Ian had shown up with his pretend friendship and his accusations founded on the same scraps of information that had led Rink's other staffers to believe the worst about me—that I'd seduced him. That it was the only explanation for how I'd "wormed" my way into his inner circle so quickly. They couldn't accept that it had to do with my brain and my easy grasp of policy. No, to the Ivy League elites I'd worked with, only the tawdriest explanation made sense, and they assumed I'd left because Rink dumped me.

Those rumors would have followed me for the rest of my career in Washington politics. So I'd left. Not just Rink's office—I'd left DC behind entirely. Its cynicism. Its corruption.

The way it devoured the reputations of good people.

I would have to wait out Ian, let him leave before I reclaimed the garden. And I'd have to hope that he wouldn't spread his poisonous lies to Miss Lily before he left.

I went back to scraping tile, but I'd only been at it a few minutes when a knock sounded at my door. I pulled out my phone and checked my doorbell app. I didn't have much fear about living in

Creekville, but I'd installed it to ease my dad's worries about me living alone and "isolated" out in the country. The only thing I'd used it for up to this point was spying on the hummingbirds who came to visit the feeder I'd placed at a perfect angle for the camera to capture. But now, as Ian's face appeared on my screen, I thanked my dad's overprotectiveness. I slid my phone into my pocket and went back to work. No need to answer the door.

Ian knocked again, but I only scraped harder. When I didn't answer a third knock, he rang the doorbell in a series of three quick buzzes.

"Brooke?" His voice was muffled through the heavy wood door. "I know you're in there. I see your car in the driveway."

"Go away," I muttered even though he wouldn't hear me.

He rang the doorbell again. "Brooke, I'd like to talk to you."

No, thanks. I pulled out my phone and fiddled with the app for a second. My dad had said...oh, there it was. I pressed the intercom feature. "As long as it's you knocking, I'm not home. Leave, Ian."

He jumped at my voice. Very satisfying.

"Brooke, I owe you an apology. Can we talk?"

"No. I have too much to do. Go away." I wasn't dumb enough to put any faith into a so-called "apology" by someone who'd ambushed me with ugly accusations on the pretext of a "getting to know you" dinner.

"House stuff? I'll talk while I help. Open up?"

"No, thank you. Now please leave before I call the sheriff."

"I really am sorry, I promise. I'd like to explain what went wrong and make it up to you."

Yeah, right. "If the sheriff doesn't scare you, maybe your grandmother will. Should I call her?"

He hesitated, leaning his head against the doorframe for a second before turning to meet the doorbell camera eye to ... lens? "No, don't do that. I need to confess to her myself." He took a step toward the steps but paused again. "I really am sorry, Brooke. I was wrong about you."

Then I watched him leave until he was out of camera range.

Well.

He sounded like he meant it. Maybe I should have let him in?

But then I remembered his smooth charm through the first part of dinner last night before he'd sucker punched me.

Nah.

Good riddance, Ian Greene. He'd return to the city on Sunday, and I'd get my garden and Miss Lily back.

CHAPTER ELEVEN

Ian

Gran watched me walk into the parlor without a word, her cocked eyebrow telling me she was waiting.

"Brooke doesn't want to talk to me," I told her. "I don't think she'll come out to the garden again until I'm gone."

"You want to tell me what all this is about? You take a phone call in the middle of our conversation, disappear next door, and come back looking like a kicked puppy. And Brooke Spencer wouldn't kick a puppy even to save her life. So what's going on?"

"I've been kind of an idiot," I admitted, collapsing to the sofa next to her. "A big one. I was worried she was trying to prey on you because you're ol…" I trailed off when her eyebrow rose even higher. "Because I saw some red flags," I amended. "So I started digging into her background, and on the surface, what I found confirmed my suspicions."

Gran's look shifted to incredulity. "You investigated my *neighbor*? What is *wrong* with you?"

"It didn't look right," I said, feeling both sheepish and grumpy. "Sweet woman shows up next door and suddenly you're talking about leaving her your very valuable property? I wanted to make sure she was legit."

"And what did you find?"

"All the right pieces. I just..." I sighed and rubbed my hand over my face. "I put them together completely wrong."

"So you're saying you've discovered that my neighbor is a sweet young woman and nothing more?" Gran's tone was dryer than the Sahara.

"Not exactly." Brooke had more layers to her than I'd expected, an integrity I hadn't seen in...years. "But she's not a con artist. Anyway, I made some accusations last night that I needed to apologize for. Since she wouldn't answer, I tried shouting them at her through the door. That was not super effective." I rubbed my face again. Had I forgotten how normal people behaved? That genuinely good people existed?

Apparently. I felt more idiotic by the minute.

Gran sat next to me and patted my back. "I suppose it's time for a confession of my own."

I dropped my hands enough to give her a sideways glance. "Come again?"

"This is only about eighty percent your fault." She looked thoughtful for a second. "No, eighty-five. But the rest is probably me."

I straightened and scooted into the sofa corner so I could study her more closely. "This should be interesting."

"You know you don't come around here often enough."

Leave it to Gran to keep me humble with a scolding even as she led into some kind of "confession." "Stipulated," I said.

"And you also date women who are totally wrong for you."

"Gran..." But she held her hand up for silence and I subsided with a small sigh.

"You do."

"You haven't met any of them."

"That's how I know," she said, unruffled. "If any of them were something special, you'd be bringing them around. What's more, if they were truly right for you, they'd make you bring them around because they'd want to know where you come from. How you became you."

I nodded. Fair enough. I'd never had the slightest interest in bringing any of my girlfriends out to meet the family.

"But Brooke is perfect for you."

"Gran..." This time there was a note of warning in my tone.

"Hush. I knew you wouldn't believe me when I told you. And it didn't work to flat out ask you to come and visit me so I could casually introduce you. So I'm the one who was up to no good in this whole scenario, not Brooke. I lied about considering changing my will because I figured it was the fastest way to lure you here."

"Gran!" That one was pure shock.

"I know." She had the decency to look guilty for a split second. "But to be fair, I expected you to be a good enough judge of character to sense her natural goodness the second you met her. Isn't it your instincts that make you such a good investigator? How was I supposed to know this would be the first time they'd fail you completely?" She crossed her arms over her chest, her expression defiant and a touch cranky.

It was such an unusual expression from her that a laugh escaped me. "I'm sorry, Gran, but you look like Izzie did when she broke your lamp that one time." Izzie was my younger sister.

The corner of her mouth twitched. "I do not."

I copied her expression and posture, crossing my arms.

Her twitch turned into a reluctant grin. "You look ridiculous."

I lifted an eyebrow.

"Oh, fine," she said, uncrossing her arms. "I'm sorry, Ian. I shouldn't have lured you down here. Next time, I'll nag you relentlessly until you come to visit, *then* I'll force you to get to know my pretty, single neighbor. Will you forgive me?"

I leaned over and hauled her tiny self into a hug. "On one condition," I said into the soft, white curls tickling my chin.

"What's that?" she mumbled into my chest.

"Help me figure out how to apologize to Brooke?"

She slipped out of my hug to stand and hold her hand out to me.

"Oh, that's easy," she said, pulling me to my feet. "As long as you're ready to do hours and hours of back-breaking work."

I grinned down at her. "Is a trip to your place ever complete if I don't?"

"Come on, you stinker," she said, keeping her hand in mine as she led me out of the French doors. "We've got some repenting to do."

CHAPTER TWELVE

Brooke

"I will not hide in this house."

I said it aloud, to no one. I just needed to hear it. It was late Saturday afternoon, and I needed some dinner. Or linner. I needed whatever it was you ate when it was hours past lunch and too early for supper.

I could eat one of my freezer meals. But what I really wanted was the meal I'd almost gotten to eat last night at Caps until Ian opened his big mouth and ruined everything. He was still doing it. Thinking about the dinner he'd deprived me of was ruining me for any dinner I might eat now. *Darn* that man.

"You don't get to ruin linner, Ian Jerkface," I informed the kitchen before calling to place an order for takeout from Caps. Maybe I should stop and get a dog or cat while I was in town too, so I could at least pretend I was talking to another living soul instead of myself.

Maybe a cat? I'd never had an animal growing up. I wasn't even sure which type of animal person I was. For all I knew, I might be a secret hamster lover. "Maybe I should start with a fish?" I asked the kitchen. It didn't answer.

I peeked through the front window again. The BMW still sat in Miss Lily's driveway, but I wasn't going to hide inside just because I didn't want to deal with her devil-spawned grandson.

Keys in hand, I marched out to my car but saw no one, and it was a relief to back out of the driveway without having to tell anyone to go away.

When I picked up my dinner from the restaurant and set it on the front seat of my car, the late afternoon sunlight streamed through the windshield. My soul rebelled at the idea of eating it alone in my poorly lit kitchen.

Pendant lights, I decided. The kind that lit everything but washed it in a soft, warm glow that spoke to the kitchen as the soul of a home. I'd have to ask Grace for a good electrician and spend some time with lighting catalogs, but the thought excited me. Replacing Uncle Fred's outdated dome fixture would be one more way of making his house my home.

But for right now, I wanted to enjoy the outdoor time I'd missed in the garden with Miss Lily. I thought for a minute before putting my little SUV in gear and heading for Folly Creek. There was an informal park beside it, a few picnic tables on a small open patch of bank that locals had set out years before.

I parked and settled myself at the table nearest the babbling water then I tucked into the meal I *should* have had last night. As with everything else, Miss Lily had been right about the stuffed mushrooms. Well, everything but her grandson, Detective Disrespectful.

There were few things truly delicious food didn't make right, I decided as I finished up the last bit of risotto. I was gathering up the trash to bring home and toss when the alert went off on my doorbell app, making my stomach flip. I had no doubt who was on my doorstep.

I opened it to find Ian on the porch, Miss Lily next to him. He held a hand-drawn sign that read, "I'm really sorry. I hope you like the flowers," while Miss Lily waved cheerfully.

Then when I didn't say anything, Ian looked down at his grandmother and shrugged. She only answered him with a smile and a pat on his arm before leading him from the porch and out of sight.

What was that about? I squinted at the app but couldn't see any flowers. Puzzled, I drove home, curious against my better instincts to figure out what Ian's note had meant. Had he left me a vase of flowers?

But no. I was wrong. Very wrong, I saw as I pulled into the driveway. Four large planters fired with a beautiful blue glaze now lined my front walk. I recognized them as the expensive showpieces from Grace's garden section. Each burst with dahlias, zinnias, and begonias. It was a dazzling display.

I hurried to the front door and found a card tucked inside the frame.

Hi, Brooke.

I'm sorry. I guess it's a job hazard for me to see fraud where there is none. I spoke with Ellen Brown. You're the real deal. It should have been enough for Gran to vouch for you, but I'm very protective of her. I'm sorry I dug into your past. It was none of my business.

I asked Gran what I could do to make it up to you. She said you've been too busy with school to put in the flowers you wanted so you were waiting until next year, and she suggested I do it instead. I planted them in these tubs so I can take them away next weekend if you don't want them. I thought it was safer than digging up your yard and putting them in.

When I asked Gran what your favorite flowers were, she said I should guess based on what I know of you. So this is my best guess. If I'm wrong—and why would I be right at this point?—I will happily replace them with different flowers next week.

With sincere regret,
Ian

I stared out at the flowers again, then walked back down the path, stopping to study each ceramic tub. The flowers were perfectly spaced and arranged with a good eye for color, all except the zinnias which were a riot of color as zinnias should always be. I wondered if Miss Lily had tutored him in all of this. I could sense her fine eye in their display.

But if he had also chosen the *types* of flowers himself, he'd succeeded in picking all my summer favorites. It must have taken him several hours. The intensity of the project was exactly why I'd put off doing it myself until next year.

I reached the end of the walk and turned to study the effect. It was lovely. All four pots lined one side of the walk, and while I would have staggered them with two on either side, other than that, they immediately brightened the yard and made it more inviting.

Ian's car was still parked in Miss Lily's driveway. I considered for a split second going over to say thank you, but the stress of his accusations was still too fresh. I'd endured much of the day with that acidic feeling in my stomach that had characterized my final month in the senator's office, and I wasn't ready to deal with the man who'd brought that back after two years.

But Ian *had* meant his apology. Even if Miss Lily had pressured him into making it—I sensed he wasn't used to being wrong—I could also sense his sincerity, and DC had taught me to value sincerity above everything.

I wandered back up the path and let myself into the house. I would forgive Ian. No question. I just needed time.

CHAPTER THIRTEEN

Ian

By Sunday morning, there still wasn't a peep out of Brooke. She hadn't texted or come over to Gran's. But she also hadn't smashed her new planters or pulled out the flowers, so maybe that was something?

I didn't want her to feel like she had to hide in her house all day again because of me, so after breakfast on Sunday morning, I packed my bag, dropped a kiss on Gran's head with a promise to return soon, and drove back to DC.

The whole way I hoped Gran had been able to talk Brooke back out to the garden.

Brooke was still on my mind Monday morning when I sat in on the partner meeting while they discussed strategy on a huge case we'd taken on for a chemical company in trouble for pollution violations. We'd be representing them in the negotiations while working with a lobbying firm to fast-track a Senate bill that would decrease the penalties for their type of pollution, thus lowering their financial exposure in a settlement.

These were the kinds of tactics that often annoyed me about the firm. I preferred to do the work of exposing corrupt politicians and lobbyists, not digging up more ammunition to arm their cause. But that was politics. Everyone spent time on both sides of the ball. It was how things worked.

Except for Brooke, maybe. If Ellen Brown was to be believed—and I did believe her—Brooke was a purist in a sea of cynics. According to Ellen, Brooke had been too good for this world. *My* world. The world of backroom deals between major players. A world where the fates of entire industries were decided over long, boozy lunches so long as everyone got their back scratched.

On Tuesday, I woke up and reached for my phone, hoping there was a text from Brooke acknowledging my apology and maybe even forgiving me. There wasn't.

Wednesday, I wondered about her again as I returned to the arboretum for another meeting between the VP and the lobbyist. This time I wore a ball cap and flip-flops as I strolled past them to drop an "empty" soda cup in the trash next to them. It contained a mic so I could pick up their conversation. The quality wouldn't be great, but it would be enough to confirm or refute my suspicions.

Ha. They would be confirmed. I had no illusions. But as I passed a bed of flowers like the ones I'd planted for Brooke, I wondered whether she'd liked them or not. When Gran had told me to choose species I'd thought Brooke would like, I'd reminded Gran that I didn't know Brooke. So then Gran told me to pick flowers that reminded me of Brooke, and I'd get it right. That had been easy. I chose the most vibrant ones I could find, with lots of petals and color.

"Begonias," the sign in the flower bed read. Terrible name, but the flower had felt right for her.

By Thursday dinner time, I was wondering if maybe I should go back to Gran's this weekend, see if Brooke had kept the pots. I could ask Gran, but she'd tease me. Although... it wasn't like she wouldn't see through me when I showed up for the third weekend in a row. And I *had* mentioned to Brooke that I would be back.

I was dithering, Gran would say. And I wasn't a ditherer. Hadn't ever even used the word before suddenly becoming one. Which forced me to confront the truth: I'd grown interested in Brooke on her own merits. I hadn't been interested in a woman in a good while, finding the last few I'd dated to be almost...interchangeable.

I winced at myself for even thinking the word. That was my fault for not getting to know them better. But they'd all had the same highly polished, coolly professional edge, and the conversations on the first couple of dates had all centered on their jobs—mine too—and DC gossip. I hadn't left any of my second dates interested in asking for a third.

But Brooke had walked out on our first dinner before it was even served, and I had *so* many more questions about her.

No, *for* her. I was done asking other people to explain Brooke to me. I'd go to the source from now on.

Guess that meant I was going back to Creekville, even if it meant enduring Gran's teasing.

A text vibrated my phone and I scooped it up, hoping it was Sherrie with a lead on one of our cases, but it wasn't Sherrie's name on my screen. It was Brooke's, like thinking of her had summoned her. Her text was a simple, *Thank you for the flowers.*

I hesitated, thinking about what to say back. Finally, I tapped out, *No problem. Least I could do. Sorry I got it so wrong.*

There was no quick response. No typing dots. I woke my screen a few times, hoping I might have missed a text, but there was nothing.

"You are turning pathetic," I said out loud. I got up and went to brush my teeth before I put my pathetic self to bed. My phone vibrated with another text, Brooke's name flashing from my bathroom counter. I snatched it up, toothbrush still in my mouth.

Miss Lily confessed she misled you. I think I understand how you could draw all the wrong conclusions.

I grimaced and spit out the toothpaste. Another text came in.

Like, EVERY wrong conclusion. All of them.

I grinned. She wasn't short on what Gran would call "moxie." I texted back. *So you're saying...more flowers?*

She answered fast. *You should invest in a nursery, probably. Maybe a whole flower farm.*

I searched for Gran's favorite florist in Creekville and placed an order online for delivery the next morning. It would have to do until I could deliver the next bouquet myself, because I was *definitely* going to Creekville this weekend.

CHAPTER FOURTEEN

Brooke

I opened the door to a delivery person obscured behind an enormous spray of blue hyacinths.

"Delivery for Brooke Spencer?"

"That's me." I accepted the vase. "Who are these from?"

"There's a card included, and the tip's been taken care of," the young man said. "Have a nice day, ma'am."

He jogged back to his van. He was a teenager, maybe one of my new students starting Monday, working his last day of summer break.

I whisked the flowers into the kitchen and settled them on the island, immediately injecting some life into the room. I suspected they were from Ian after our texts last night, but I plucked the card from its plastic holder to double check.

"A stalk for every wrong assumption I've made about you," it read. "I called *a lot* of people."

I didn't know whether to laugh or snort at the six separate hyacinth stalks packed into the sleek square vase. I tapped out a quick text to him. *Got your flowers. You're short at least three.* I smiled as I imagined him reading it. Ian Greene was by no means my favorite person, but Miss Lily or his parents had definitely drilled him on how to do proper apologies.

I gathered up my teacher bag, a large tote that brimmed each morning with new whosits-and-whatsits for my classroom, grabbed my keys, and was halfway to my car before I went back and grabbed the flowers too. Those could come to work with me today.

At school, I stepped into my classroom and took a deep breath. I loved the smell of it. Smell was probably my favorite sense. I loved the sharp tang of weeds slipping loose from the soil in Miss Lily's garden. I loved the musty odor of sawdust with each new mess I made in my house. I loved the scent of this classroom when I walked through the door each time, a mixture of the bulletin board paper on the walls that kind of smelled like sawdust too. Maybe that was what gave this room the feeling of home.

I studied the wall displays. One section showed all the major organ systems in the human body. Another section gave the taxonomy of the blue-footed booby, a goofy-looking bird from the Galapagos Islands that did indeed have blue feet. It would help the kids learn classifications. Another section showed famous women biologists, and a fourth —smaller, but important—gave information about vaping and showed the effect on human lungs.

Today I would have only half the day in my classroom. The rest would be filled up with faculty and department meetings, and like yesterday, probably lots of the other teachers popping in to welcome me to Lincoln High School and offer help with anything I needed.

My room was in good shape going into Monday. The white boards were filled with the daily science standard we were working on, interesting science facts, and an inspirational quote, all in my neatest handwriting. I'd been wishing I'd found my way to teaching sooner, but maybe I was glad I'd come along in the whiteboard era and not the dusty green chalkboard one.

The rest of the day went exactly as I expected, meeting new teachers whose names I remembered using memory tricks I'd read about and planned to use for memorizing my students' names. I sat in a faculty meeting where we reviewed the school objectives for the year, then a department meeting where everyone complained about their chronically underfunded labs. But they all sounded excited for the new year, ready to be back, ready to get to work.

This was exactly the kind of environment I thrived in, but I couldn't shake a feeling of impending doom. For three nights in a row, I'd had stress dreams. In one, I'd spent the whole night filing papers and woke up feeling like I'd already spent a whole day at work. In another one, I showed up to discover the office had switched my classes at the last minute, and I was supposed to teach calculus instead of biology. Last night had been the worst of all: a rerun of a high school dream I'd had of going to school in my underwear. It was so much worse doing it as a teacher.

I should feel so good about Monday and my first day of teaching, but I couldn't tell the difference between my excitement and my nerves. I took a long glance around the classroom again. Everything was exactly as it should be. Crisp new folders waiting to receive student work, lab desks polished free of fingerprints, walls bright and inviting.

Most days I would stay and rearrange, tweak, straighten. But today, on this last Friday afternoon before students came, what I needed most was to get out of the classroom and give myself some garden therapy, digging in Miss Lily's soil and letting my senses take over to chase the anxiety away.

I scooped up my now-empty tote bag and paused at the door to survey the classroom one last time before turning off the lights.

Ready or not, Monday was coming.

I really, really hoped I was ready.

"They're coming along," Miss Lily announced from the end of the tomato row.

"I'm excited," I replied, touching one of the fruits. It was turning orange, soon to deepen to red. "How much longer?"

"A week, I think. Your tomato sandwich is almost here. Maybe I'll make you one to celebrate finishing your first week of teaching."

"Can't think of a better way to celebrate surviving it."

"Did I use the word 'survive,' girl? I did *not*." Miss Lily gave the final "T" some extra oomph. "I said celebrate, period. There will be no surviving. Only thriving. Like the tomatoes."

I smiled at her. I appreciated the vote of confidence, but I suspected that it had been so long since Miss Lily's very first week as a teacher that she may have forgotten how overwhelming it felt.

"Don't think for a second that I'm forgetting how overwhelming it is," Miss Lily continued, and I felt a slight thrill of terror that Miss Lily could read my thoughts. "Every first week is unnerving until you're about twenty years in. But what I *do* know from my years of long observation are the telltale signs of a teacher who has what it takes to succeed. You want to know the only thing that might trip you up from having the school year you hope for?"

"Yes, please." I definitely wanted to know but also felt kind of disappointed that any such thing existed. I was hoping the dread of getting it wrong was just my anxiety talking.

"Your dread of getting it wrong."

This time, I stared at Miss Lily, my mouth slightly open in surprise. "Are you…can you read my thoughts?"

Miss Lily gave a big, happy laugh. "No, child. Not in the way you think. That's experience speaking from talking many new teachers through the process over the years. You want everything to be perfect. It won't be. If you measure yourself against perfection, you're always going to come up short. Does that make sense?"

"Yes, ma'am." It wasn't the first time someone had talked to me about my perfectionist tendencies.

Miss Lily walked down the row and stopped in front of me to smile. "What experience gives you is perspective. By the end of the year, you will have a much better yardstick for measuring success. You'll have a better sense of how much your students can do and what standards to hold them to. My best advice is that those expectations should always force them to stretch in ways they don't think they can because that's how they grow. But you definitely should *not* measure progress against the ideal you have in your head at the moment."

Miss Lily leaned over and rustled the tomato plant nearest her for a minute, pushing back the leaves to expose a misshapen tomato. "Look at this, and then compare it to the one right next to it. You see how that one is shaped like every tomato you buy from the market?"

I nodded. I did see, and I saw where Miss Lily was going with all of this too.

"You know which one is going to taste better when we slice into them?" Miss Lily asked.

"They'll taste the same?" I guessed.

"They'll taste exactly the same," Miss Lily confirmed. "So we'll have grown two perfect tomatoes even if they look different."

"I'll keep that in mind," I said.

"No, you won't," Miss Lily grinned. "Not until about the late spring, and then you'll remember I said this, and it will make more sense in the context of your classroom. You'll be exhausted and dying for the year to be over, but also completely excited for the next school year to begin so you can implement everything you'll have learned by then."

"I can't tell if that's overwhelming or encouraging," I said.

"Both," Miss Lily said, her eyes twinkling. "You've got what it takes, Brooke-girl. Hang in there. You'll be fine."

We settled down to do more weeding, working in companionable silence save for the chatter of birds and Miss Lily's soft humming. Miss Lily tended toward happy hymns, and this afternoon was "For the Beauty of the Earth," a good fit for the peaceful garden.

We'd been at it for almost an hour, moving on to the bean plants and then the carrots, when the sound of a car door closing nearby stopped Miss Lily's humming.

"Well, well, well," she said, smiling, without even looking toward her driveway.

"Are you expecting someone?" My heart had started an odd skip-beat, knowing it was probably Ian.

"Always and never with this one," Miss Lily answered, and before I could ask what she meant by "this one," Ian appeared at the end of the row.

Unlike the previous week, he was dressed casually in gray shorts and a blue T-shirt that looked like the kind of soft only a thousand washings could get you.

"Hey, Gran. I see you roped Brooke into being your unpaid labor again." He wrapped Miss Lily in a hug that made the petite woman grin.

"Good to see you, handsome grandson. What brings you out this weekend?"

"Wait, just 'handsome grandson'? Can I be 'most handsome grandson'? I mean, have you *seen* Landon lately?"

Gran laughed. "All of my grandchildren are unreasonably attractive, talented, and intelligent. But again, to what do I owe the pleasure?"

There was a sly glint in Miss Lily's eyes, one I was growing to know meant she was angling to do some mischief. Probably some misguided matchmaking. I was about to interject and change the conversation in case Ian was on board with Miss Lily's scheme, but he spoke instead.

"Mary promised me Mississippi roast again if I came out this weekend, and it's not like I was going to turn that down."

"Smart boy," Miss Lily said. "Now help us pull these weeds."

Normally, the space between rows was cozy to me, tucked in between the bean vines. But the idea of Ian kneeling in the dirt with us suddenly shrunk it from cozy to claustrophobic.

"I've got it," I said. "It's no big deal. Why don't you two head in and visit while I finish up here?"

"Are you sure you're all right if I go in?" Miss Lily asked. "I don't want you to feel overwhelmed."

"It's no problem," I assured her.

"Then I think I'll go get myself some sweet tea while you two finish up out here."

"That's not what I..." I trailed off because Miss Lily had already beelined for the house as if she hadn't heard me.

Ian laughed and settled on his heels beside me. "Give up," he suggested. "She's had eight decades to get that wily."

I smiled. "I'm figuring that out. You know what you're doing out here?"

In answer, Ian plucked five weeds in quick succession and displayed them on his palm. "Yes, ma'am."

"Well, it's not that hard when the tomato plants are already so big." There was something about Ian's sureness of himself that always made me want to bring him back down to size.

"Don't worry, I can do it when they're seedlings too. Gran kept us busy every summer out here. She called gardening the cure to 'hooliganism.'"

"She thinks gardening will cure everything, as far as I can tell," I said.

"She's usually not wrong." He flashed me a smile and turned his attention to the weeds, already moving down the row to the next section.

Not to be outdone, I picked up my pace, wanting to get out of the garden and away from awkward small talk as quickly as possible. But Ian didn't engage in any small talk. He worked at his weeds quietly, and when I sneaked a glance at him, his face was relaxed, as if he had found the same Zen headspace I often did out here.

After several long minutes of silence, I felt a tickle somewhere inside, maybe in my chest, urging me to speak and break it. I tried to ignore it, but it didn't go away, so I cleared my throat and waded in. "Hey, Ian? Thank you again for the flowers."

"Least I could do." He sounded mellow and didn't look up from the weeds. Just kept tugging them out.

"You didn't have to," I said. But I didn't mean it. It really was the least he could have done after pulling up my past like he was yanking out those weeds.

"Of course I did." He twisted so he faced me, both of us still kneeling in the dirt. "I'd like to do more if you'll let me. All that investigation told me is that I definitely don't know you well enough to figure out what might help me make restitution."

He meant it. That was Miss Lily's influence coming through. His sincerity allowed me to drop my guard in a way I hadn't since he'd first shown up in the garden in a designer shirt and expensive loafers.

"It's okay. For real." I brushed my wrist against my forehead to catch a bead of sweat at my hairline. "I guess I hoped that all that stuff would go away once I left DC behind, but I can understand why you were being so protective of Miss Lily. I just think she can handle herself better than...well, anyone I've ever known."

Ian gave a small laugh. "True enough. You'd think I'd have learned not to underestimate her at this point."

I climbed to my feet. "I think I'm done out here for now. It's been a long day already, and I have another one ahead of me. I need to eat a big dinner and fall asleep way too early."

Ian rose too. "Gran said you start your teaching job on Monday. Still getting ready?"

"No. I'm as ready as I'll ever be, which isn't very ready." I swiped at another bead of sweat. "Tomorrow I need to do more renovation stuff. It's hard but mindless work, and sometimes that lets my brain problem-solve other things. Maybe tomorrow night I'll fall into bed with my backsplash tiled *and* brilliant new lesson plans."

"Why don't you come over for supper?" Ian said. "We can at least feed you before you go unconscious."

I waved away the offer. "That's sweet of you, but I don't want to intrude on your time with Miss Lily. I'm too tired to be good company anyway."

He nodded. "Understood. But, um..." He squinted at me and pointed to his own forehead. "You've got some dirt."

I removed my glove to reach up and rub the spot that he'd indicated. My fingers came away dirty. "Did I get it?" I asked, wiping my fingers against my grubby work shorts.

"No, here," he said, walking toward me. "You kind of spread it around."

When he was in arm's reach, he stopped and reached toward my forehead, slowly enough for me to duck away, but his presence wasn't at all threatening, so I stood still to let him get at the dirt.

He brushed at it lightly but only frowned at the results. "Uh, may

I...?" He plucked at the hem of his T-shirt, but I wasn't sure what he was asking, so I only blinked at him. He lifted it up, exposing a flash of his well-defined abs before they disappeared from view as he used the fabric to rub gently at my face. I was too preoccupied by the effect his abs had on me to squirm away from his fussing. I did notice that his shirt was as soft as it looked before he dropped it and stepped back, all so quickly that I didn't get another glimpse before his shirt fell into place.

"I don't think I fixed it," he said. "Sorry. I think I made it worse."

How dirty was my face? I'd need to wash it in the kitchen sink where there was no mirror to make me die of delayed embarrassment.

"It's fine." I scooped up my gardening tote. "I'm going home anyway. Enjoy your dinner."

"Thanks," he said. "I will."

I refrained from touching the spot he'd tried to clean, sensing without looking that his gaze was following me to the front door. I closed it behind me then leaned against it. Ian had cleaned dirt off my forehead, and I'd started wondering what it would be like to make out with him.

What even...?

I touched the warm spot on my forehead. That was no fever. That was Ian Greene's touch causing the heat reaction, and as an expert in biology, I knew we were dealing with chemistry.

And I had no interest in that kind of chemical reaction.

CHAPTER FIFTEEN

Ian

Gran had warned me that Brooke was an early riser, so I knocked on her door with a mug of Mary's hot coffee in hand a half-hour before a time most people would consider decent.

Sure enough, Brooke opened the door already dressed in paint-stained work clothes, her hair gathered into a braid.

"Hey," she said, a look of mild surprise on her face. "What's up?"

"I don't know if you've heard the rumors, but I love tiling so much. So I'm hanging around on your front porch hoping you'll let me help."

Her eyebrow rose. "You love tiling floors?"

"It's my favorite. So relaxing."

She rolled her eyes. "Your gran talks too much."

I grinned. "So can I help?"

She hesitated for a minute. "I can handle this by myself."

"I brought fresh coffee. Letting me help will be like letting me get free therapy." I extended the mug.

She accepted and stepped back. "All right, if it's really going to make you happy."

"Wildest dreams come true, I swear." That earned me another eyeroll, but this one came with a laugh.

"I'm tiling the stupid downstairs bathroom. It's tedious. I don't know how it can do anything besides frustrate you completely, but sure, jump right in and swear at the grout with me."

"Wait, can I see the library before we start?"

"Sure," she said, turning toward it. "I like how it came out."

"It's pretty great," I said from the threshold, admiring her progress. Bookcases now lined the walls, though only one of them had any books in it yet. Several boxes sat in front of each bookcase bearing labels like, "Cooking," "History," "Fiction," and other genres. A large, overstuffed striped chair sat in the corner beside an end table holding a blue glass lamp. "This isn't the kind of space I would picture when I think of a home library, but this makes me want to curl up and read and the kind I would usually picture doesn't."

"That's the goal," she said. "I wanted a quiet place for reading. Cozy, comfortable."

"You nailed it." The bookcases were white against the soft neutral walls, and the reading chair was teal cotton instead of leather and brass tacks. The light and airy vibe felt like Brooke, like she'd translated her personality into the room.

"Thanks. But there's no rest for the wicked. Or dummies who buy old houses. Come on."

I followed her to the bathroom, noticing the other changes she'd made since I'd last been inside. She was obviously leaving the small foyer for last. It still sported old wallpaper and outdated light fixtures, but the walls leading upstairs had been freed from the faded floral wallpaper and given a coat of the same paint from the library. The room opening off the right of the foyer already had new paint, baseboards, and refinished flooring too.

"What will this space be?" I asked, pausing at the doorway of the empty room.

"Not sure yet. Maybe an office. I'm not big on formal living rooms, so I'd just as soon have any company come visit me in my TV room or the kitchen." She moved up the hall leading out of the foyer and paused. "This is the guest bathroom. It'll be a tight squeeze, but I think if I climb into the tub and work from there, we should be able to both fit."

I joined her at the doorway and realized immediately that she had been humoring me when she'd allowed me to join her. The space was too small for both of us to work comfortably. I'd be underfoot, but I didn't want to give up and go home. Not after I'd imagined a day of working with her in the house. Making up for my suspicion of her. Getting to know her.

"I'm not going to crowd you into the bathtub just so you can give me something to do. Is there anything else you've been wanting to tackle? I want to help for real, not get in your way."

"Anything else I want to tackle? That's a long, long list," she said with a sigh.

"Give me the most annoying job on it, the one you're dreading doing." I'd much rather hang out where she was and work, but I liked the idea of being useful somewhere in her house more than going back to Gran's to get spoiled while Brooke overworked herself alone.

"I mean, they're all the jobs at the bottom of my list for a reason," Brooke said. "They're the worst jobs that I haven't been able to force myself to do."

"I'm game," I promised. "Send me in, coach."

She cast a doubtful eye at me. "I mean the *really* bad jobs."

"You know what I do for a living, right? I dig up the worst kind of dirt on the worst kind of people. There is nothing in this house that can be worse than that."

"Oh, really? How about removing wallpaper?"

"Tell me what to do. I haven't done it before, but it can't be that bad."

Brooke answered with a snort. "Wait here. I'll get the stuff. You just uttered famous last words."

She disappeared down the hall and I heard the back door open. I Googled "how to remove wallpaper" while I waited for her. The process didn't look too complicated. And I hoped she would assign me the foyer and hall. That way we'd be working next to each other.

She came back a few minutes later with a plastic painter's tarp, a paint scraper, and an oversized spray bottle. She set them down and dug a small object from her back pocket. "This will score the wallpaper," she said, handing it to me. "Lay down the tarp, then run this down the wallpaper but not too hard or I'll have to putty it before I paint. Then peel it off and let it fall to the tarp. It's disposable, so I'll bundle it up and throw it all away."

"Doesn't sound too bad."

"Oh, you sweet, innocent man. This is going to suck. You can tap out anytime you want to because there are a hundred better ways for you to spend your Saturday, and all of them start with you running away fast."

"I can handle it." I flexed as a joke but caught an appreciative glint in her eye before she shook her head.

"It doesn't take strength, it takes patience. So much patience. Wheelbarrows of patience. Most of the paper won't come up very easily. Once you've peeled away everything you can, there's still going to be patches that cling to the wall like they were welded there. But let's get you through the initial removal first, and if you survive, I'll explain how to do the next part."

She laid the paint scraper in my hand and turned toward the bathroom, but I reached out to catch her fingers and hold her in place with a light pressure she could break with no trouble.

"I'm patient, Brooke. I won't tap out."

She glanced down at my hand holding hers and slowly slid hers from my grasp. "I know I don't teach English, but I'm almost positive there's some subtext there." She ran her freed hand down her braid, pushing it behind her and meeting my eyes. "If you're here to help, I'm happy to have it. But if you're here for anything else…"

"No ulterior motives, I promise. Just trying to make up for digging into your business."

"The flowers were enough," Brooke said.

"They weren't. I'm so used to having to do metaphorical dirty work that I couldn't see the obvious when it was right in front of me. I won't make that mistake again. And I figured the best way to atone is to do your literal dirty work. You're doing me a favor by letting me."

She shook her head. "All right, if you really want to. I'll be cursing at tile if you need anything."

She disappeared into the bathroom. I decided to start on the wallpaper closest to her. "Brooke?" I asked, as I looked for the first seam to begin ripping.

"Yeah?" She was only a few feet away even though I could only see the soles of her shoes. She must have already knelt to do her work.

"Why Lincoln? And teaching high school? And this old house?"

She was quiet for a while. Finally, she said, "In college, I wanted to go into biology because I find life so interesting. I like looking at the building blocks of it, understanding how it all works. I ended up on a career detour after I lost a friend, and—"

I waited, but she didn't continue. "Brooke?"

She crawled backwards out of the bathroom and sat on her heels in the hallway, watching me for a few seconds. "How much did you find out about my past in your investigation?"

"Ellen Brown set me straight on a lot of it," I admitted. "But I'd like to hear about it from you."

She seemed to consider that for a minute before disappearing into the bathroom again. Just as I wondered if she'd decided to ignore my question, her voice floated out to the hall.

"I wanted to make a difference. I thought I'd get into research, find a cure or two." She laughed. "Like it's that easy. Anyway, my roommate died from using a faulty vape. I kept telling her not to vape at all, but she insisted it was way better for her than smoking. Then she got a lung infection, and she didn't recover. I took a semester off because her death was this reminder that life was really short, and I wanted to make sure I was making it count."

"And you decided politics was the answer? I think that brings a lot of idealists to DC."

"No, I wasn't interested in politics. But I felt like I'd failed Chelsea, my roommate, because I couldn't talk her out of vaping. So I decided to make it harder for the vape industry to hook young people, and I spent my semester off researching the industry, the growth rates, the demographics of users. It was disturbing. I wanted to make sure no one else on my campus would become their victim either by getting sick or losing someone like I did. And I started lobbying my state delegate to get a law passed that banned the sale of flavored vape products in Virginia, since that's how they hook new users. They were pretty much marketing straight to kids."

"And that's when you caught Ellen Brown's eye?" I asked.

Her head popped out of the bathroom. "She's great, isn't she?"

I nodded, and she disappeared again.

"She convinced me to do an internship with the delegate's office the following summer," she explained before giving a soft but audible curse.

"You liked it that much, huh?"

"Sorry, no, I can't get this tile piece to line up right." She fell quiet for a moment, then I heard a small, satisfied grunt, and she picked up the thread of the conversation. "I did like working for the delegate. And I thought if I brought my science background to work with me in her office, I could do some good work around all kinds of related issues. Public health, the environment."

"So you got into politics like thousands of idealists all over the country."

"Idealism isn't a bad thing."

"I didn't say it was."

She poked her head out. "Your tone did."

I thought about it. "I think we need idealists. But reality is hard on idealists. When I come across a newly arrived true believer on the capital scene, ready to devote their lives to public service, I already see the impending slow-motion wreck of their ideals unfolding in their future."

She rose and walked far enough out of the bathroom to lean against the wall and study me. "And it makes you cranky."

It wasn't a question. The characterization made me yank extra hard at a piece of wallpaper. "Cranky is for old people. I'm not cranky."

"Which word should I use? Cynical?"

I ripped another long strip of wallpaper away as I considered the number of young political staffers I'd seen bruised and sometimes beaten by the reality of Washington politics. "Tired. It makes me tired."

"Why stay?"

The question startled me into pausing and looking straight at her. She was studying me, her head tilted slightly, like I was a microscope specimen. "Why stay in my *job*?"

"You sound like you hate it. Just quit." She disappeared into the bathroom like she hadn't suggested something completely farfetched.

"It's not that easy."

"No," she agreed, her voice slightly muffled. "But it *is* simple. You make a decision, and you walk away. It's making the decision that's the hard part."

"I know you're speaking from your own experience, but it's not easy *or* simple for me," I said. "Besides, I don't want to quit."

"So you stay and get crankier, working inside a system you hate."

"I don't hate the system," I corrected her. "I dislike the way a lot of powerful people game it."

She was quiet for a long time before answering. "Me too."

I knew she must be referring to whatever had happened with her and Senator Rink, and I wanted to say something comforting. Or at least something that condemned the predatory creep. But she hadn't specifically brought up the assault, and we didn't have the kind of connection that gave me the right to comment on it, no matter how well-intentioned.

Time for a change of subject. To what?

"So removing wallpaper does kind of suck." My segue was about as subtle as the loud chipping I was doing with the paint knife.

"You can go home any time," she said cheerfully.

"I didn't say I wanted to." It miffed me that she was still ready to dismiss me. I'd only managed to peel away a little of Brooke's exterior,

KISS ME NOW

making less headway with her than I had with the wallpaper, and I was now equally invested in both projects. "You didn't say why you bought your uncle's place."

"I fell in love with it," she said. "I had a chance to stay here for a couple of months when I was going through a rough patch, and something about Creekville spoke to me. I think it's the opposite of DC in every way, and it came at exactly the right time."

"I don't know about that." I kept my tone light. "Gran is always full of gossip about the old guard in town, and I get pretty regular rundowns on the political drama of the mayor and city council."

Her answering laugh made me smile. "You got me there. But I guess the difference is that everyone here is genuinely trying to make Creekville better, not get their personal slice of the pie. I've heard people talk about a sense of community, but this is where I've felt it. This town is the real deal."

"Gran loves it," I acknowledged.

"You don't?"

"I don't *not* love it. I've enjoyed it when I've been in town. But mostly I come here to hang with Gran, so even though she's lived here my whole life, I guess I don't really know the town that well."

"I'm still learning it too, but I can tell you some things I know."

"Go ahead, shoot."

"Everyone smiles," she said. "They all say hello. And once you've done business with one of them, they know enough about your story to bring it up every time after that. But it's a good thing. Like when I bought a can of paint at the hardware store and Grace asked what I was working on. Now she's my unofficial renovation consultant. Or Bixby's Bakery. Taylor Bixby knows my order as soon as she sees me walk through the door, and it's ready at the register before I say a word."

"What's your order?" I asked. "Wait, no. Let me guess." I considered her low-key style of dress, her drink preference the night at Gran's house, the simple tastes she'd shown in her renovations so far. "Americano," I guessed. "And a blueberry muffin."

She appeared in the hall. "How'd you know?" Then her expression fell. "I guess that's a pretty boring order, isn't it?"

"It's not that. I'd describe it as classic."

"I think what you're saying is that I'm predictable."

"No." I studied her, taking another inventory of her fine features, the light wash of freckles across her nose, her healthy summer glow. "You are anything but predictable."

A tinge of pink rose in her cheeks and she disappeared into the bathroom.

"I'm getting something different tomorrow anyway," she called. "I don't like being predictable."

"Let me guess, you're going to switch it up with tea and a scone?" I laughed when she gasped and her head popped back out. "Don't be so shocked. I do this for a living. I kind of have to know how to profile people. You do start to see patterns in types of people, but it doesn't make you predictable."

"It's literally exactly what predictable means. You're able to predict what I'm going to order at the bakery and then predict what I'm going to switch it to." She was quiet a second. "Actually, that's creepy. Instead of talking about how I'm lame and predictable, let's talk about how it's very suspect that you can do this."

"It's not," I protested with a laugh. "It's more like…think of that Sherlock series with that one guy, Benjamin Cummerbund, and—"

"Benedict Cumberbatch," she corrected through her laughter.

"Right, that guy. The point is, it's all just observation, deductive reasoning, and a working knowledge of human nature. I'm not creepy, I swear."

"It's creepy."

I took a few steps until I was in front of the bathroom and sat on the floor. "Brooke," I said, to her well-shaped butt.

She started and twisted around until she sat facing me. "See? You just creeped up on me. Now you're literally creepy."

"I did not creep up on you. I walked over. It's not my fault if I move with the grace of a ninja."

She reached out and plucked a piece of wallpaper clinging to my hair. "Yes, picture of grace."

"I'm not creepy. It's possible that I may have seen your coffee cup with your order written on the sleeve sitting on your kitchen counter last time I was here, and it's also possible I noticed a basket of teas next to the sink and guessed that scones are the right thing to eat with tea."

She looked mollified for a second. "Wait, but it's weird that you remember that a week later."

"Not for me, it isn't. It really is a job hazard. My brain catalogues this kind of thing. Sometimes it's annoying, but mostly it's helpful. Sherlock Holmes," I said, pointing at my chest. "Are you less creeped out?"

"That you were snooping on the contents of my kitchen?" She didn't look reassured.

I wasn't sure where to pivot here. I'd meant to show off a little. *Of course* it would read as totally creepy to a single woman living by herself. I opened my mouth to apologize, but she broke into a grin.

"I'm kidding. You're not creepy. That all makes sense. I notice stuff like that at people's houses too. I'm not sure I buy your Sherlock Holmes claims given the fact that you got me totally, utterly wrong, but I definitely concede that you aren't a creepy dude."

"Thank you?" I wasn't sure if I'd been complimented or insulted.

She flashed a cheeky grin that did nothing to clarify the issue and turned back to her tiling. When I stood to go back to my wallpaper, I caught a glimpse of her progress. She only had about two feet left of the bathroom, and then I hoped she'd come join me on the wallpaper project.

We worked in easy silence for the next hour as more of her slowly emerged from the bathroom as she filled in the tile, crawling backward as she went. I could almost guess how much tile she had left to lay based on how much of her appeared, bit by slow bit, until finally only her head and shoulders were inside the bathroom. At last, she backed all the way out and stood, glancing over the tile with a sigh that sounded very satisfied, like when I finished a full set of bench presses at a new weight.

"Done?" I asked.

"Yeah, come see."

I joined her in front of the doorway and peered in. The bare concrete foundation was now covered in a pattern of small interlocking black and white squares. With the grayish blue—or was it blueish gray?—paint she'd chosen and the light gray vanity, the bathroom looked like a designer had done it.

"Nice," I said as she stepped back to study it from beside me. "It's both contemporary and timeless with an airiness that invites some rest."

"Timeless? Airy?" Brooke tilted her head to study me. "Is this another Sherlock Holmes thing, to be into interior design?"

"It's possible Gran talks me into renovation show marathons."

"Chip and Joanna or the Property Brothers?"

"Chip all the way."

She stretched her arms overhead and reached way up before dropping them and shaking them with a sigh. "I think that's it for today. I find it's best to only do one major project in a day or I burn out."

"But I didn't make much of a dent in the wallpaper." I wasn't ready to leave yet, I realized. I liked working near her, even in silence.

She waved her hand. "It's okay. That's two hours less labor that I have ahead of me now. I appreciate it, but you're forgiven. No further repentance required. Go hang with Miss Lily with a clear conscience."

"I don't mind," I said.

"At this point, I'd be taking advantage of you. Seriously. Make your grandma happy. I'm going into town for some other supplies."

"All right. If you're sure." *Don't be sure*, I willed her. *Make up some other job for me to do.*

But instead she gave me a cheerful, "I'm sure," and led me to the door.

"See you around," I said from the bottom of the steps.

"Bye," she said and had the door closed before I'd even turned toward Gran's house.

It bothered me as I crossed her yard to Gran's place. It wasn't that she'd been rude. She'd been relaxed, the edge of annoyance I'd felt from her disappearing altogether by the time she'd finished tiling. It was more that I didn't seem to register with her at all, like she'd quit thinking about me before she'd even got the door shut, her mind on other things.

It didn't sit right, especially not since she'd taken up most of my free thoughts for almost two weeks now.

By mid-afternoon, it still nagged at me. I'd taken Gran to lunch and enjoyed the conversation with her as I always did. We'd watched a couple of cooking shows together, and then Gran excused herself to take a nap, and suddenly I had the afternoon yawning before me, but it was all cluttered up with thoughts of Brooke.

What was she doing right now? What kind of supplies had she run into town to get? What was she going to do with the sitting room she hadn't touched yet? Was she giving herself a break? She started work on Monday, and she probably needed to give herself some downtime before diving into her first day of teaching.

She probably wouldn't slow down as much as she should. My investigation had painted the clear picture of a woman who was a go-getter.

I needed to invite her to dinner. That way, she could enjoy a nice meal and easy conversation before the school year started.

I crossed to her yard again, my step light, thinking about where I should take her. Somewhere with a great view. Good views were always relaxing. I knocked as I considered whether I should choose something casual or if she'd be up for a change of pace.

She opened the door and gave me a puzzled smile. "Hi. Did you forget something?"

She had changed into clean jeans and a UVA T-shirt. Her hair looked faintly damp, like it was still drying from a shower.

"No. Well, yes, I mean." I shifted my feet. I sounded like an idiot. Or like I was twelve. Same thing. "I forgot to ask if you'd like to get dinner later. Maybe a do-over at Caps where I behave like a normal person and we get to enjoy the food."

Her puzzlement didn't clear. If anything, she looked more confused. "Are you asking me on a date?"

I almost said no, but I had never been a coward. I wasn't going to play this off with an excuse. "Yes, Brooke. I'm asking you on a date. For dinner. I promise not to apologize for anything or do anything I need to apologize for."

That got me a slight smile. "That's really sweet, but I meant what I said earlier. Or didn't quite say, I guess. I don't have time for anything besides work and this house right now, and that includes dates."

I was surprised by the rejection and immediately felt stupid for being surprised. Why shouldn't she tell me no, considering what I'd put her through? Did I really think I was such a prize that she'd overlook all of that for a dinner invitation?

No. But I had sort of thought I'd sensed a vibe between us while we worked.

I must have waited too long to process my own idiocy before I answered, because she gave an awkward laugh.

"I'm sorry," she said. "I hope that didn't offend you. It's not you. It's just my life right now, I promise."

I held up my hands. "Whoa, no explanation necessary. I should be the one apologizing for putting you on the spot. I just thought..."

"You thought..." she prompted me when I lost the right words.

"Nothing." I smiled, hoping she sensed that it was genuine. I hadn't been wrong about our vibe. I was sure of it. But I could respect that the timing was off for her. "You don't owe me any explanations. Sorry again for putting you on the spot. I hope this won't make it awkward for you to come by Gran's when I'm around."

Her eyebrow went up. "Since you're barely ever here, I'm sure it will be fine." But unlike the other times she'd made the same pointed criticism, her tone was teasing.

"That's going to change," I said. "Gran's trick worked. Scaring me down here *did* remind me of how much I love being here. Need it, even. It's good to feel grounded, and that's how I feel when I come out here."

"Good," she said. "I'm sure Miss Lily will love having you around more."

"I think so," I answered. "She says she will, anyway. I better get back over there. Maybe she'll be my date tonight."

I left with a wave and a smile she couldn't see because I had a plan now. I would absolutely respect her no dating boundary, but I was going to make sure that Brooke began to look forward to my weekend visits as much as Gran did.

CHAPTER SIXTEEN

Brooke

Monday morning, I walked into Bixby's Bakery a half hour early, nervous to start my day and not at all sure a jolt of caffeine was a good idea. But the routine already felt important to me.

"Good morning," Taylor called. "Order coming right up."

A minute later, she met me at the register and handed me an Americano and a blueberry muffin.

"Thanks, Taylor."

"First day on the new job, right?" Taylor asked. "You nervous?"

"Extremely," I said, pulling out my wallet. "But trying to have a good attitude."

Taylor held up her hand. "This was already covered. Good luck today!"

I paused, my wallet half out of my tote. "What do you mean it's covered?"

"I mean a mysterious benefactor paid for your morning coffee and muffin and asked me to wish you good luck."

"Oh. Well, I'll pay it forward. The next two coffee orders that walk in are on me." I laid a bill on the counter and turned toward the door but stopped. "I have to know. Was it Miss Lily?"

Taylor grinned. "Close. Definitely Miss Lily's genes."

Ian, then. I took a sip of the coffee, made the way I liked it. "That's what I get for being predictable, I guess."

"Sorry?" Taylor said.

A smile tugged at my lips. "Nothing. If you have a way of getting in touch with my mysterious benefactor, tell him I said thank you, and it was a great way to start the day."

I drove to school, sipping the coffee and smiling at Ian's gesture. I was grateful for something else to think about instead of obsessing over how my first class would go.

Inside my classroom, a spray of flowers greeted me from my desk, but it wasn't the same bouquet I'd gotten from Ian. These were peonies, full and luscious in vibrant shades of pink.

For a moment, I wondered if these were his doing too, but whoever had put them there had keys to my classroom, so it couldn't be him. It was early still, and from the mostly empty parking lot, I suspected I was one of the first teachers on campus. Maybe these were from the administration, wishing me good luck? Or the PTA? It seemed like a PTA thing to do.

I plopped my brimming tote on the desk and plucked the card from the profusion of petals.

Dear Brooke,
I hope your first day is nothing but happy surprises.
Good luck!
Ian

I studied the wild bunch of peonies. How had he gotten these in here so early? I was leaning down to smell them when my principal walked in. "Good morning, Ms. Spencer. Saw your light on and thought I'd check in to see if you're ready."

"Thanks, Dr. Boone. I am. I think." Then deciding it wouldn't do for my boss to think I was uncertain I added, "No, definitely. Looking forward to the students arriving."

"Good, good. Looks great in here. Stop by my office any time if you need something." She left with a cheerful wave, and I broke into action, unpacking the books I'd lugged from home, some of my favorites that I would set out for kids to read if they finished classwork early.

The next hour was punctuated first by visits from other teachers wishing me well, then by the slowly increasing sounds of locker slams and chatter as more and more students arrived on campus. Finally, at 8:25, the warning bell rang to give the students five minutes to find their homerooms. I took a deep breath, propped open the classroom door, and stood beside it, ready to begin my new career.

The first two periods went by in something of a blur, but an okay one. I didn't butcher anyone's names too badly, they all seemed curious about their new teacher, and only one kid in second period looked like a potential class clown. By third period, I had the pace down enough that I was able to give them the last ten minutes of class to take a Harry Potter sorting hat quiz to identify which Hogwarts house they belonged to, then find the taxonomy for their mascot.

I slipped behind my desk and took my first deep breath since I'd opened the classroom door, and the faint scent of the peonies tickled my nose. I hadn't even had a chance to thank Ian for them yet, or the breakfast either. I'd do that on my lunch break.

They were too pretty to resist, and I leaned forward to sniff the one closest to me, but as my nose grazed the petal, I caught a deeply unsettling movement from the corner of my eye. The immediate sense of wrongness told me exactly what I would see when I turned my head. I had a sixth sense for spiders, and there it was: one largeish white spider which was somehow even more horrifying than the brown ones that regularly lurked in my house. But it was so much worse than I expected because there was also a stream of small ones.

So many small ones. Dozens. Hundreds? I froze, but a small squeak came out of me, enough to turn the heads of the students nearest my desk as the first of the tiny, white peony-spawned devil spiders skittered toward me across the desk.

I shoved back from it with a yelp and plastered myself against the wall, watching in horror as still more baby spiders tumbled from the peony and spread out on my desk.

"Miss?" asked the young man nearest my desk whose name I couldn't remember in my frozen brain. "Everything okay?"

I tried to answer him, but my mouth only moved in silence, no words coming out. I managed to point a shaking finger toward my desk. He and the two other boys closest rose and came around to investigate the problem.

"Whoa," one of them said.

"What's wrong?" asked a girl in the class, her voice nervous.

"Spiders," the other boy announced.

"So many," the first one said in awe. *Justin.* His name came back to me.

"A buttload of spiders." That was…Kyle?

I swallowed and tried to pull myself together. "Don't say buttload, Kyle."

"Uh, right, Miss Spencer. Um, that's a boatload of spiders."

I should probably say something funny about how "boatload" wasn't a scientific measurement, but all I could do was inch down the wall away from the spiders. *Pull yourself together, woman*, I ordered myself. But myself did *not* listen.

"Can you boys…" I waved in the direction of the spiders.

"I got it," said a girl from across the room. She hurried over to the desk. "Oh. These are crab spiders. We get them in our garden. They rarely bite."

"Rarely?" repeated Kyle, also backing away.

"Justin, grab a paper and kind of sweep them in here," the girl said, plucking up my can of freshly sharpened pencils and dumping them out on Justin's desk.

He complied and picked up the index card where I had written my carefully rehearsed welcome speech for each class, using the stiff edge to send all the tiny spiders into the pencil cup, finally sending the mother spider to join them.

"I think we got them all," the girl said, crouching to study the desk more closely.

The panic in my chest loosened, and I stepped away from the wall but also far away from my desk. I wasn't going near those flowers again.

I crossed to the front of the room and cleared my throat before addressing the class. "I don't love spiders."

"No kidding," one of the boys muttered, and the other kids laughed.

"I, uh, normally handle them better than that. I just didn't expect to see a giant one crawl out of a flower right in front of my face."

"Why not?" asked the girl—Hailey, I finally remembered—holding the cup full of spiders. "That's where a lot of them like to live. You're pretty scared of bugs for being a biology teacher."

I swallowed. I could feel myself walking a delicate balance here. I needed to figure out how to cement my authority as a biology teacher despite having just freaked out over spiders. If I didn't, I would lose their respect for the year, and that would make this class much harder, and probably my other classes too, if the story spread. And I had every reason to believe that it would.

"I don't love spiders," I repeated. "But I do find them fascinating. Like, for example, beneath the lens of a microscope. In fact, we'll do a whole unit on the essential part spiders play in our daily lives without us even realizing it." I had no such unit planned, but I immediately added it to my to-do list.

Hailey raised her hand. "You want me to keep these little guys for the unit?" She asked it as a dare, testing to see if I would lose my cool again.

"No, it won't be for a while yet. Better release them. Um, outside. By some bushes." I gave a slight emphasis to the last part, confident in my suggestion since there were no bushes beneath my classroom window, which meant the spiders would find a new home far enough away to give me peace of mind. "Bushes will be a great home for them."

Hailey shrugged like that was fine with her but didn't seem interested in further needling me. The bell rang to announce lunch, and I hid a sigh of relief beneath the clamor. I wished Hailey would have volunteered to take the peonies with her, but when the students cleared out, the vase still stood on my desk, mocking me as if it knew I would come no closer.

What were my options here? I *really* hated spiders. No matter where I encountered them, they never seemed *right*. They were always eerily out of place, whether it was a dusty corner of Uncle Fred's gardening shed or a flower arrangement, or even spinning a web across one of the paths I walked in the morning before the heat set in. There was no context where I'd run into a spider and thought, *Yes, this one belongs here.*

I hated them so much that I considered calling the custodian and asking him if he would mind removing the vase for me. But Miss Lily had cautioned me that the most important people for any teacher to befriend were the office clerks and the custodial staff, and I didn't want to risk alienating the janitors by treating them like servants.

That meant I could either leave the flowers be and not go near my desk ever again as long as I lived, or...I could put on my big girl panties and handle it myself.

I took a deep breath and a single step toward the flowers, but I faltered on the second step at the memory of the disgusting white spider emerging from the peony.

There was no way. None. I couldn't touch it again.

Great. Now I was held hostage by Ian's peonies since my lunch and purse were by my desk as well.

Pull it together, Brooke, I ordered myself, and this time myself tried harder. What if I could get rid of the flowers without touching them directly? I checked the trash can beside the door for the extra trash bags the custodians stored beneath each liner for easy switching out at the end of the day.

I removed one and shook it out to make sure it would be big

enough for peony/vase/spider containment. Then with a deep breath, I rushed the peonies like Elmer Fudd going after a rabbit with his net aloft, swept the trash bag over the flowers, cinched it beneath the base, and jerked the whole mess upright while dancing back from the desk in case I'd missed any spiders.

I didn't see any of Satan's beasties on the desktop, and if any remained in the peonies, my death grip on the garbage bag would make sure they didn't escape. I whisked it out of my classroom and went looking for one of the large campus garbage cans to dispose of it, but each one I passed still felt far too close to my classroom.

I finally reached one near the outdoor basketball court that looked to be the last possible garbage can where I could drop the peonies, and I flung the trash bag in and pivoted toward my classroom, ready to eat my lunch and get ready for my next class.

"Hey, there," a male voice called behind me, one that didn't sound like a sophomore.

I turned and spied one of the PE coaches. He was new this year too, and I racked my brain for his name but couldn't come up with it. I'd been introduced to so many other teachers during the in-service meetings last week.

"Hi. Used your garbage can. Hope that's okay."

"Depends," he said, coming closer. He was only about 5'10 but he had the broad, square build of a wrestler, and it made him seem taller. "You're the new science teacher, right? Is this some kind of *Breaking Bad* scenario where you're cooking meth on your lunch break in your class lab and disposing of the evidence?"

I held up my hands in the universal sign for "you caught me." "Meth cleverly disguised as spider-infested peonies."

"Smart," he said, a smile tugging at his lips. "I'm Noah Redmond, by the way. The other new kid. PE and wrestling coach."

I accepted his outstretched hand for a shake. "Are we the only two new teachers this year?"

"I think so. Want to form an alliance?"

"What are we doing in this alliance?"

"I'm thinking it's mainly an alliance where we have lunch together sometimes so neither of us has to sit alone as the new kid."

I pretended to think. "How do I know that if I say yes, I'm not accidentally choosing the loser table?"

He laughed. "Let me see if I got this right. Between the science nerd and the jock, you're worried that *I'm* the one at the loser table?"

"Those are fighting words, Mr. Redmond."

"That's scary coming from the local meth dealer. Would it help you feel better to know that my undergrad degree is in human anatomy and I love comic books?"

It was my turn to laugh. "So what you're saying is that you're actually the huge nerd?"

He grinned. "That's what I'm saying."

"I've always liked the nerd table. Lunch sounds great."

"I'd say join me in my office because it's big, but it has the disadvantage of smelling like boys' gym socks."

"Drop by my room anytime," I offered. "It doesn't smell like gym socks. But, uh, how do you feel about spiders?"

He shrugged. "I have no strong feelings about them."

"Then you should definitely come by my classroom any time for lunch. Bring your own Lunchables."

He grinned and gave me a mock salute before disappearing into the gym.

I smiled all the way back to my classroom. My hopefully spider-free classroom. I'd made a new friend. A funny one. I dug out my salad and cell phone from my tote and took a seat far from my desk just in case. Then I settled down to figure out how to politely thank Ian for the peonies that now decorated the bottom of the most distant trash bin on campus.

CHAPTER SEVENTEEN

Ian

My eyes flickered toward my phone as it vibrated. I normally never checked it when I was in a meeting with a partner, but I'd been half-expecting a text or something from Brooke once she saw the flowers. But the screen showed Gran was calling, and I sent it to voicemail. I'd call her back when the meeting was done.

Keep your mind in the game, dude. The stern talking-to only sort of helped. I tried again to focus on what Don Schill was saying.

"This will be delicate," the older man said. "But if there's a sitting senator with skeletons in his closet, he deserves to be exposed."

I nodded. "Isn't there always a senator with skeletons in his closet?"

"Fair point. But usually they're shoved so far back that we can't get to them. This time, my gut says we'll find something."

Normally, this would be when the partner who called me in would give some disclaimer about how our sometimes shady work was doing a greater good. One of the things I liked about Don Schill was that he didn't try to dress up his motives.

"Rink is a particular lowlife, and it'll give me great pleasure to bring him down. But also, it'll make us a ton of money," Schill concluded.

"We're going after Rink?" I repeated. Schill hadn't mentioned the specific senator before, but I wasn't surprised to hear Rink's name. I'd gone pretty far out of my way to plant some information with a lobbying firm that wanted to block a tech regulation bill Rink was sponsoring.

"Yeah, it's Rink," Don confirmed. "Slippery devil, but I've got faith in you. Can you handle it?"

I gave a grim nod. "If there's something to find, I'll find it."

"All right, then. Here's what the client has given us so far. I'd like end-of-day reports starting tomorrow, no paper trail."

"You got it, sir." I scooped up the folder and returned to my desk. I didn't have to look at the file to know Rink was dirty. Whatever Rink's dealings with Brooke had been, he'd been entirely in the wrong. A couple of mornings spent with Brooke doing home renovations were enough to convince me of that. Now that I could see past the suspicion Gran had planted, it was clear that Brooke was a woman of character.

It reminded me that I owed Gran a return call.

"You've stepped in it now," she said as soon as she answered.

"Uh, what?"

"Brooke is one of the most sensible young people I've ever known but she has one unfortunate weakness: an irrational fear of spiders."

I held the phone away from my ear for a second to study it, as if that would somehow make more sense of Gran's words.

"Gran, I feel like you're starting a story in the middle. Can you back up a bit?"

"Those flowers you sent her," Gran said. "They were a thoughtful touch except for the part where they were full of spiders. And Brooke hates spiders."

A sinking feeling struck my stomach. "I definitely didn't order spider-filled flowers. Is she okay?"

"I expect so, but I'm not certain," Gran said. "I didn't hear this from her. I don't think she'll even be home for a few more hours. But I asked Nancy, the attendance clerk, to keep an eye on Brooke for me. She's the one that dropped the flowers in her room for you. Word is all over campus that there was an unfortunate spider incident in Ms. Spencer's third period class, and that she walked all the way to the other end of campus to throw out a bouquet of flowers. So I'm guessing she either really hates you, or the flowers you sent her were the source of the spiders."

I groaned. "I can't get it right with this woman."

"Interesting that you keep trying," Gran said, her tone sly. "Why is that?"

"Because you did such a scarily good job of convincing me that she was a scammer that I haven't been able to apologize enough to her since!"

"And that's important to you?" Her tone was still sly.

I declined to answer.

Her laugh came across the line. "Smart boy. But it's not my fault you read her so wrong."

"Gran. It's one hundred percent your fault I read her so wrong."

"No, you did that because you're jaded. Anyone who spent his time around decent folk all day would have seen right through to Brooke to her solid core, not found a grifter." She laughed again. "Come on, admit it's funny that you got her so wrong."

"Too soon," I grumbled. "And now I've made it worse. This is becoming a pattern with her."

"Then break it," Gran said. "But maybe not with spider peonies. Will I see you this weekend?"

"I'm not sure," I said. "I got a new case, and I think the partners want this one expedited. I'll come if I can."

"It'd sure be a lot easier for you to smooth things over with Brooke in person."

I imagined spiders crawling out of flowers and shook my head. "I somehow doubt that. But I promise, if I can, I'll drive out."

I hung up and pulled the Rink dossier closer, but instead of opening it, I reached for my phone. I searched long and hard before finding the perfect gif to send Brooke, a little animated spider wearing a sombrero and doing a dance.

A half hour later, she sent a reply. *How did you hear? I haven't even told Miss Lily.*

I smiled and tapped out a response. *Like a spider, I have a lot of eyes.*

I regretted it immediately and regretted it even more when she replied.

Like a spider, I find that super creepy.

I sighed. *I know. I heard it as soon as I sent it.*

A minute of silence passed, and I texted again. *I'm sorry about the bouquet. Wasn't my intention.*

Don't worry, she answered. *I know. They were pretty until the spider thing. But I still have the ones from last week, and those make me smile.*

A goofy little wave of warmth traveled through my chest at the thought that I'd made her smile. *As penance, Bixby's is on me tomorrow too.*

OH GOOD, she replied. *WILL BE GETTING A HUGE CHOCOLATE ÉCLAIR AND FANCY COFFEE.*

I laughed, sensing I was forgiven. *You deserve it. No more flowers.*

Sherrie poked her head in. "Did I just hear you laugh?"

I set my phone down. "Yes. But Schill has a new case for us, and there's nothing funny about it. Have a seat, and we'll dig in."

Sherrie and I spent almost an hour poring over the Rink dossier. There was a factual accounting of the bills he'd sponsored and passed, the hearings he'd conducted as the chairman of the powerful appropriations committee, the commendations he'd won over the years. On their face, they painted the picture of a shrewd but fair legislator, committed to sound fiscal principles, honorable in the execution of his office once he'd put the scandal of his old extra-marital affairs behind him. He'd often worked with senators across the aisle to pass laws in the almost-forgotten tradition of an era past.

But.

The whisper network told a different story: the story of a man whose behavior in private was a betrayal of his constituents' faith. And I'd learned that the whisper network rarely ever got it wrong.

I pushed the folder away and leaned back in my chair to think. "Are you familiar with the term 'whisper network'?" I finally asked Sherrie.

"Sure. It's pretty much always subordinates gossiping about their superiors, yes? Like servants in the old days in mansions, or actresses in Hollywood warning each other about predatory directors."

"Yeah. The kind of thing that can't be discussed openly because the predators are savvy enough to skirt the rules in a way that makes it hard for accusations to stick. Or because disclosure means the whistleblower risks losing their job."

"What do you see in Rink's file that makes you think the whisper network will have some info?"

"Nothing concrete." I pinched the bridge of my nose as I considered the feeling in my gut. I trusted my instincts, and they were telling me that Rink was dirty. But a hunch wasn't proof. "I think Rink came to Washington as a young senator and treated the social scene as his personal hunting grounds, lining up a string of conquests. When that caught up to him and the scandal threatened his re-election, he did the talk show apology tour, cried that he was sorry, and promised to reform."

"You don't buy it," Sherrie said.

"I don't buy it," I confirmed. "Why does a guy like that, married with a high-profile job, even have affairs?" I knew the answer. This was a test to see if Sherrie did.

"Childhood wounds, maybe. Power, definitely."

"Bingo. Rink likes power. To him, seducing women is part of that. That instinct doesn't go away because you're caught."

"It just finds a new hunting ground?"

"Yep." My voice was grim as I thought about what Brooke must have gone through to only be getting back to work now, two years after her time working for the senator, and in a totally unrelated career. How many more young women had been victims of the senator before her and even since?

"So you think that Rink settled with Brooke Spencer to buy her silence about an affair?"

My eyes snapped to Sherrie's. "I think it's worse than an affair. That's why it's time to check in with the whisper network."

"Wait, boss. You had me looking into her *before* we caught this case. It's an awfully big coincidence that we suddenly get to investigate Rink, isn't it?"

"What have I taught you about coincidences, Sherrie?"

"That there are none." She gave me a long look. "You're a little bit scary."

I gave her an easy smile. "Only if you're a bad guy."

She answered with a low laugh. "All right, then. Teach me how to crack the whisper network."

For the next half-hour, I showed her how I'd combed through the Spilled Tea blog then met with Brandon himself to confirm my suspicions. But I also showed her how to comb through social media for staff photos from years past in Rink's office, then to trace the women pictured through social media posts, sifting for clues that any of them may have had the same experience that Brooke did.

"I'll reach out to his former chiefs of staff to see if I get anywhere with them, but chances are slim," I told her. "They have a lot to lose by speaking out if they were aware of this kind of behavior during their time on his staff."

"But you think this kind of thing definitely went on?"

I considered the question. "The alternative is that Rink put his predatory tendencies on ice for twenty years and Brooke Spencer was too tempting for him." In a weird way, I sort of got that. She'd had a strong effect on me in a very short time. "But the reality is, these types of impulses and patterns are pretty ingrained, and a US senator has very few people attempting to keep him in bounds. It's more likely that he grew sneaky rather than that he reformed."

"Unfortunately, I think you're right. I'm already stressed about how many more victims we'll find," Sherrie said.

"Comfort yourself that this ends with stopping him cold."

She nodded and rose. "I've got a lot of research to do."

"Keep me posted."

When I reported to Don Schill before heading home, the only

thing I could say definitively was that based on Sherrie's research, Rink had a tendency to hire beautiful, young women as junior staffers. There was nothing concrete yet, but Rink's hiring pattern alone told me that we would eventually find evidence. And when we did, Rink would pay.

CHAPTER EIGHTEEN

Brooke

True to Ian's word, when I walked into Bixby's on the second day of school, Taylor smiled from behind the counter and said, "I hear we're doing a caramel macchiato and an éclair. Great choices. Coming right up."

I smiled as I nibbled on the éclair on the drive to campus. *You didn't have to buy my breakfast again*, I texted Ian when I parked.

I really, really did. Sorry again.

I'd reassure him when he came to visit Miss Lily again this weekend that he had more than atoned. I climbed out of the car and prepared for an even better second day of school.

Day Two did not go better.

It was hard to imagine it could go worse than spider-infested Day One, and in fact, the day had looked much more promising until lunch time when Noah Redmond popped his head in.

"Offer still free to eat my lunch in here?"

"Only if you promise to amuse me with witty banter."

He winced. "Ooh, sorry, I just came off a freshman PE class, and all I have is 'your mom' jokes."

"Then come in here and eat but don't tell me any of those. Unless there were some good ones?"

We had a good lunch while we traded war stories from our first two days on the job.

"The kids are nice enough, but I don't think they're taking me too seriously," I concluded.

"Well, I actually taught before in Charlottesville, so maybe I have the added advantage of three whole years of experience to help put things in perspective?" He said it like he was asking permission to share his insights, and I liked that. Miss Lily was one of the few people who could barrel right into dispensing advice without asking because that's what eighty years of good living earned you. I liked that Noah didn't assume he should just start spouting his opinions.

"I'd love to hear your thoughts," I said.

"I guess the main thing I figured out is to give up trying to get it perfect." He smiled at whatever expression he saw on my face. "Not so easy for you?"

"No. Not so easy."

"I get it. The good news is that eventually you start to do each thing better. In the meantime, the one thing that matters most is if the kids can tell you like them. I don't mean that you want to be their friend—they'll take advantage of that like you wouldn't believe. But if they sense that you sincerely enjoy them, they'll remember that far longer than—" he flicked a glance at my bulletin boards "—say, taxonomy."

I gasped. "How dare you? Dear King Phillip Came Over For Green Spaghetti. Domain, kingdom, phylum, class, order, family, genus, species. They will *never* forget."

"You're right. I'm vastly underestimating their monkey brains. But I'd invite you to come hang out during one period of freshman boys PE and tell me you're still convinced that your memory trick is going to stick in there, much less words like phylum."

"Fair enough. Hey, I'm going to run to the ladies' room, but feel free to hang out. I'll be back in a few."

"Sure."

The high school was set up in two main buildings, each with four long corridors where classrooms were loosely situated by subject. I was the last classroom in the science wing, but luckily, the faculty restroom for our whole building was just at the other end of my hall. I passed kids sitting in small groups eating lunches, some from brown bags, some from cafeteria trays. They chattered with each other and paid no attention to me. I remembered that feeling: that teachers only existed during class and not between bells.

I finished in the restroom and washed up, giving myself a thorough once over in the bathroom mirror. I got the sense that Noah wasn't in a relationship, and while I felt more of a friend vibe with him than anything, I still wanted to look presentable in case I ever changed my mind. I verified that I didn't have anything embarrassing stuck in my teeth, and no drips or spills on my shirt. It was fitted without being tight, and I re-tucked it into my knit skirt with its cheerful polka dot print and headed back to my classroom.

By the time I reached my door, a few kids called after me, "Hi, Miss Spencer."

That was nice.

Or at least it was until I heard a giggle after one of the hellos.

I slipped into the classroom and leaned against the door.

"Noah?"

"Yeah?"

"Do you think you and I are going to be friends?"

"Sure, I think so," he said in his easy way.

"Um, I'm going to take advantage of that."

His eyebrow went up. "How so?"

"I'm going to turn around, and I need you to tell me if there's anything about my appearance from the back that would cause a hallway full of high schoolers to laugh."

"All right," he said slowly.

I turned. "Well?"

"Uh."

It was all he needed to say. "What is it?" I plucked at the back of my shirt then ran my hand over the seat of my skirt, not feeling anything suspicious.

"Your skirt. Um."

I leaned my head against the door, not wanting to face him now. "My skirt what?"

"Is sort of tucked? In?"

"No." It was more of a whisper, the last gasp of denial. I swept my hand over the back of my skirt again, this time sweeping lower. My butt was safely covered but when I got below that...

I turned back around to face him. "My butt is not hanging out."

"No."

"But it's barely covered."

"Yeah, that about covers it. Er, I mean sums it up." He pretended to study his fingernails. "I'm going to stop talking now."

I reached up and worked at the back of my hemline as discreetly as I could. The end of my skirt was, in fact, tucked into my underwear. I unstuck it and my skirt drifted into place. "It was nice knowing you, but when I leave campus today, I'm never coming back."

"Don't do that," he said. "Who else will I have to share in my humiliation over teaching half of second period with my fly down?"

I stared at him suspiciously. "Are you making that up to make me feel better?"

He shrugged. "Oh, it happened. Just not second period today. My second year of teaching. There's really not a good time for that experience. And yet I'm still here."

"What do I do?"

"Maybe walk right back out there again with your skirt straightened out and get a drink from the water fountain like nothing is wrong? It'll be less interesting for them if they think it was no big deal to you."

"Good plan but I'd rather die."

"You might. They may actually chew you up and spit you out in glee if they know this got to you."

"That's fine. Can you call the office and tell them I no longer work here?"

He smiled. "No. You got this. Get back in the game, Spencer." He pointed to the hallway.

I took a deep breath, snatched my water bottle from my desk, and walked back out. This time the kids all turned to regard me with greater interest.

"How's it going, Ms. Spencer?" one of the boys called as I passed.

"Great. Couldn't be better." I made it to the drinking fountain halfway down the hall and stood there for the eternity that it took for my water bottle to fill, a half-smile fixed on my face while I tried to also simultaneously appear lost in thought. I made the return trip to my classroom, but this time no one paid attention to me.

"How did it go?" Noah asked when I slipped back in.

"I think okay? I'll at least stay through the last two classes today. But I can't promise I'm coming back tomorrow."

He laughed and returned his chair to the nearby lab desk as the bell rang. "Fair enough. But for what it's worth, I don't think anyone saw anything."

"No, but they almost saw *everything*."

"But it's still only almost. Hang in there, Spencer."

"Thanks, coach."

He gave me a salute and headed back toward the gym.

I survived fifth and sixth periods, drove home and ate a pint of ice cream, and decided when my alarm went off the next morning that I would go back to school after all. By the time I drove home Friday, I was even smiling as I thought about telling Ian the story.

Except that by dinnertime on Friday, Ian hadn't shown up at Miss Lily's. I'd hung out for an extra-long time in the garden pulling weeds that could have waited a few days, waiting for a car—his car—to turn into Miss Lily's driveway…but nothing.

It was annoying. I was annoyed with myself for finding it annoying.

I made myself a tomato sandwich—Miss Lily had naturally been exactly right about the glory of a tomato sandwich when the tomato comes straight from the vine—and burned off some restless energy by stripping wallpaper.

I should've been exhausted after a disaster-laced first week. Instead, I was keyed up. I'd put some energy on reserve for seeing Ian without realizing it, and now that energy had nowhere to go.

Well, no surprise. I'd said no dating. And Ian had proven he was far more likely to stay in DC than visit Miss Lily. But I'd been egotistical enough to think that he'd make an excuse to come see her so he could see me.

Stupid.

He was giving me what I wanted, and that was a good thing.

"You have no time for Ian Greene," I scolded my reflection as I washed my face before bed. "You will never have time for Ian Greene. Make your to do list and go to sleep."

I woke up early on Saturday, determined to get the last of the stubborn wallpaper stripped from the hallway. Except I didn't want to. I didn't want to do anything but burrow under the covers and put on *Dream Home Makeover* and not do a single useful thing.

But the thing about owning my own house was that it was mine and no one else's, which meant the work was mine and no one else's too. I stared up at the ceiling and weighed a day-long Netflix binge against having to live with the ugly old wallpaper again.

"Do something nice for Brooke tomorrow and take care of the wallpaper today," I told the ceiling.

"Ugh, fine," I answered myself. "But I'm going to need an incentive."

Music and muffins, my brain said.

"I will strip wallpaper for one hour with my music blaring and then I can have a muffin. A chocolate chip muffin."

Blueberry is healthier.

"Chocolate chip or nothing."

My head stayed quiet, so I dragged myself out of bed and slid on cutoffs and a holey Nationals shirt, set up my Bluetooth speakers, and cued the playlist I'd used when I trained for a half-marathon right after college, a collection of rap and rock anthems so cheesy they should be used for fondue. I showed the wallpaper no mercy while singing about the eye of the tiger at the top of my lungs.

I'd moved on to a new section of the hallway and a song about big butts when a hand brushed my shoulder. I screamed at the top of my lungs and whirled with my scraper in front of me like a weapon.

Ian jumped back and put his hands up. "I come in peace," he yelled over Sir Mixalot.

I blinked at him and pressed a hand against my racing heart. When he pointed to my phone and gave me a questioning glance, I nodded, and he moved to it and turned down the volume.

"You can't walk into the house of a single woman living on her own," I told him. "You almost gave me a heart attack."

"Sorry about that," he said. "I knocked a bunch of times, but I had a feeling you wouldn't hear me over the music."

"When did you get here?" I asked.

"I only knocked for a minute."

"I meant to Creekville. I didn't think you were coming this weekend."

"Miss me?" he asked with a crooked grin.

"You wish."

"I do, actually."

My heart gave an extra beat, and I frowned.

He held up his hands, misunderstanding the frown. "I know, I know, you have no time or interest for dating. Got it. Just here to help with some renovation. And...air guitar?" he asked as Bon Jovi began singing about living on a prayer.

I glanced behind me at the mess and the sheer amount of wallpaper left to remove. Suddenly, it was the last thing I wanted to do. I wanted to say, "Forget it and let's go wade in the creek," but my busy bee setting wouldn't quite let me get away with that. "Mushrooms," I blurted.

"Mushrooms?" he repeated. "Like at Caps? Or are you into some recreational activities I probably don't want to know about?"

"Both and neither," I said. "I want to go mushroom hunting. It wasn't a super great first week at school, so I think I'm going to redeem myself by bringing in samples of different local mushrooms for them to look at under microscopes and practice taxonomy."

"I'm sure it wasn't as bad a first week as you think."

"I walked down the hall with my skirt tucked into my underwear."

A laugh tried to escape him, but he pressed his lips together for a moment then said, "Did you tell them it was an anatomy lesson?"

It wasn't funny to me yet. It would be. Scraping together a little more dignity each day as I stood up and faked calm, cool professionalism had helped reassure me that Pantygate wasn't going to be a career-defining moment. But it was going to take more than a week to be able to laugh about it. At this moment, stomping through the woods felt like a good way to beat back the lingering humiliation.

"Are you a fun guy ready to hunt some fungi?"

"Is it a thing where you become a teacher and suddenly you have bad jokes?" he asked.

"Yeah. We get a class roster and an app with joke of the day. Fungi or bye-bye."

"Fungi," he said.

I ran a glance over him. He was dressed to work in board shorts and a T-shirt with some sandwich shop logo I'd never heard of. "Let's go then. Did you drive your convertible?"

"Of course. That's the only reason I've been driving out the last three weekends. Gives me an excuse to put the top down." He grinned, and I knew it wasn't true, but I still sort of wished that he'd add a flirty qualifier, like, *And to see you, of course.*

And it annoyed me again to feel that way, of course.

"Let me grab some supplies and we'll go," I muttered. I could be honest enough to admit to myself that I had invented a reason for us to spend time together, but I didn't have to be happy with myself about it.

Twenty minutes later, I directed him to a parking lot at the head of a walking trail that wound along the creek, and we climbed out, my tote full of supplies. Instead of setting us on the trail, I led him across the bridge and into the woods on the other side.

"Hey, that bag doesn't have murder tools in it, does it?" he asked.

"It definitely does. I'm luring you out here to kill you and steal your car. Miss Lily may have some questions when she sees me driving it every day and you've been missing for weeks, but I'm smart. I'll figure something out."

"Okay, as long as I know what the plan is." He slipped the bag from my arm and slung it over his shoulder. "Teach me how to find mushrooms, Ms. Spencer."

We spent the next two hours picking our way around tree roots and discovering mushrooms on trunks, fallen logs, and hiding in the dirt. Maybe I should have felt weird about being alone in the woods with a guy I didn't know so well, but Miss Lily was good people, and despite his arrogance when we first met, I was beginning to think Ian was good people too.

He was easy company. Or, not easy, exactly. Easy company was like Noah or Miss Lily, where I felt comfortable with them right away. And it wasn't that I was uncomfortable with Ian, but there was a subtle tension there that made it something other than easy. It was a tension that wove a kind of spell that shrunk the world down to the two of us and our patch of woods. I felt it every time he took my elbow to help me scramble over a fallen log, or when I caught him watching me as I pried mushrooms loose from tree bark.

I was too smart to fall under the spells of charismatic men anymore, so I went out of my way to break it.

"Tell me about your work," I said. It was designed to remind me that he spent most of his waking hours in an environment that had been a nightmare for me. To remind me that he lived a life I'd left behind for good reason.

"What do you want to know?" he asked. "My job sounds interesting on the surface, but it's mostly Google searches and stakeouts where nothing happens."

"Then tell me about the non-boring parts of it. What's the weirdest case you ever had?"

"Probably the fish smuggler."

I stopped and stared at him. "It sounded like you said fish smuggler."

"Yep. I was trying to find some intel on a Malaysian diplomat one of our clients wanted to lobby for a construction contract—"

"By 'intel' you mean 'dirt,' right?"

He shrugged. "Potato, po-tah-to."

I wrinkled my nose. "Continue."

"Anyway, I was tailing him, and I thought I was on the trail of something big. I knew he was doing something shady. Illicit meetings, exchanges of money, stuff like that. But then I finally caught him in the act of a trade with an aide from South Korea at an embassy party. And it turns out my shady Malaysian was a dealer, all right, but in fish, not drugs. He was sneaking in a fish called an arowana and making major bank."

"So arowana, not marijuana?"

"Yeah. I turned the case over to the US Department of Wildlife and Fisheries instead of the DEA. They're pet fish and in huge demand all over Asia, but they've been banned here forever. So Mr. Malaysia was supplementing his humble government salary in the pet fish black market."

I stared at him. "You're making that up."

He pulled out his phone, tapped it a few times, and handed it over.

"Hang on, I want to sit to read this. Give me a boost." We were standing beside a fallen trunk so thick it came up to my hip, even on its side. Ian put his phone back in his pocket and wrapped his hands around my waist.

"Hold my shoulders," he said, so I did. His shoulders were as firm as they looked, and taking them put our faces at eye level, but I pretended to be interested in the tree behind him instead of meeting his gaze. There was a tiny pause before he lifted me up so I could sit on the trunk. Then he handed me his phone and the article.

It took a second to focus on it. A couple of my synapses had fried when he'd picked me up. Dang, he was strong. I swallowed and blinked to clear my head before I could read the article.

Sure enough, there was a headline about a diplomat being sent back to Malaysia in disgrace after he was busted for fish trafficking.

I cleared my throat to break the loaded silence that had fallen between us. "So you're saying stalking mushrooms in the woods with a relative stranger isn't even the weirdest thing you've done."

"Not by a long shot. But 'relative stranger'? I'm not sure that's accurate." He leaned against the trunk beside me, resting his forearms on the mossy bark, and glanced over at me with a smile. His voice was low and warm, and the tone was so inviting that I knew I needed to change the subject.

"What kind of cases do you normally work in DC?" I asked, turning to the screen again.

"All the ones you'd expect. We're in charge of a lot of oppo research."

I grimaced down at the phone. "Oppo" was meant to tank political campaigns or torpedo deals.

"What's that face?" he asked.

"Nothing." My cheeks warmed at being caught.

"Something. Tell me." He nudged me with his shoulder, an invitation to meet his eyes. It was a terrible idea, but I turned my head and did it anyway.

"You don't approve of airing dirty laundry?" he asked. "Maybe people shouldn't do bad things so they don't ever have to worry about them coming to light."

I felt weirdly vulnerable, staring into his eyes with him barely a foot away from me. I pretended to dust something from the cuff of my shorts as an excuse to break the connection. "No, I get that. I even agree. But it grinds you down after a while."

"Is that why you left DC?"

How much did he know about why I left? It was hard to say. It sounded like he was thorough at his job, and when he'd been looking into me, he may have found enough clues to form a picture. But I doubted it was an accurate one.

I picked my words carefully. "I left because after spending all that time in the metaphorical dirt, it's refreshing to only deal with the literal kind." I held up my fingers speckled with dark soil.

"Maybe our work isn't so different," he said, crouching to pluck one of the beefsteak polypores from the bag at his feet. "We're both hunting parasites."

I stared at the dull red mushroom in his palm, then met his eyes.

"No, Ian. I think it's important to remember that you and I are as different as we can be." It was extremely important for *me* to remember that. Ian might be fun in the short-term, but when I did get school under control and had the time and energy to consider dating, I'd be thinking long-term. There was no long-term for us, not with him rooted so deeply in DC.

"Are we that different though? Maybe we should build on what we have in common."

"Like what?" I asked.

He straightened and stood in front of me, his thighs brushing against my knees. "Like how I like science too. But I'm more into chemistry."

I blinked at him. "I want to make fun of you for that incredibly cheesy line."

"But you won't?"

My breath felt shallow. "No. I may have had the same thought a time or two. And because I'm curious about where you're going with it."

"I was thinking right here." He reached out and brushed a finger across my bottom lip, a feather-light touch.

It was sexy. Dang, Ian. "That seems like a good place to go." It was a bad idea. Such a bad idea.

His eyes darkened. "Does it?"

I swallowed. "Yeah." No. But not a single one of my molecules wanted to move.

He stepped between my knees and my hand snaked out to grab the front of his shirt, gathering it in my fist and pulling him closer.

"What happens next, science expert?" he asked, his voice low and a little rough.

"You shut up and kiss me now."

He closed the short distance between us, his lips meeting mine, soft at first, but a wave of need swept over me out of nowhere, and I let go of his shirt with a slight gasp and started to pull away, shocked by the feeling.

He watched me, his eyes heavy and dark, waiting to see what I would do next. I should jump down from the trunk and take myself home. Instead, I slid my arms around his neck. He drew me close and kissed me again, and I had the sensation of melting as I returned it. This time when he drew away for the tiniest second, I protested, but his mouth covered mine again, his lips warm and sure as they nudged mine apart to explore.

Every rational thought disappeared as I wrapped my leg around his waist and his hand slipped beneath my knee like he wanted to keep me there. I pulled him against me tighter, kissing him back with the same boldness.

The woods grew quiet except for the sound of blood rushing in my ears and a few soft appreciative sounds from Ian. I protested again when he pulled away slightly, but it was only to press kisses along my jaw, and I let go of him, leaning back on my hands to give him better access to my neck.

"I had no idea," he said quietly before pressing a soft kiss to the hollow of my throat. He tugged lightly at the neckline of my shirt so he could trail kisses along my shoulder.

"No idea…?" I couldn't focus.

"No idea that you would taste this good." More kisses. "Feel this good." He slid his other hand beneath my other knee and pulled lightly, sliding me even closer. But as much as I wanted to surrender to him, the soft scrape of the trunk against the back of my thighs brought me to my senses.

This was…no. This was not the right time, and it was definitely the wrong guy.

"Wait," I said, straightening and pressing against his chest. He stepped back immediately.

"You okay?" His eyes and voice were concerned.

"No. I mean, yes. I'm fine. I…this isn't a good idea, that's all." I slid down from the trunk.

"Did I do something wrong?" Now he sounded confused. I got it. I was confused too.

"Nothing. You didn't do anything wrong. It's just that…" *That I have never had the sensation of wanting to drown in someone, and I'm a little freaked out.* "That's not what I brought you out here for. I think…" I looked around, disoriented, until I caught sight of my tote. "We should get back to biology. Meaning mushrooms!" I hurried to add when I saw the glint in his eye.

And I scooped up the bag and almost sprinted for the trail, not even checking to see if he was following.

CHAPTER NINETEEN

Ian

Brooke shut down again. I could almost feel it like a physical sensation, a wall going up between us. Kissing her had felt like the one time I'd gone skydiving, but now it was as if that jump had ended in a crash landing.

The blood still surged in my temples, and I took a deep breath to settle my body down as I followed behind her on the trail. "Should we talk about that?"

"No." She crouched by a stump to examine it for mushrooms. "We definitely aren't going to talk about that."

"Got it." I could use some time to process the fact that I'd just made out with Gran's hot neighbor in the woods, and she had blown my mind. I picked my words carefully. I didn't want to make her feel like she had to retreat even more. "Change of subject. You grew up near DC?"

"Yeah. Virginia suburb. You?"

"Not really. Baltimore."

She looked up at me. "Baltimore is almost as close to DC as McLean is."

"Yeah, but it's more its own city than a lot of suburbs are."

"I feel like I should defend McLean against that slander, but it's true, to be honest. The whole point of McLean is for everyone who works in DC to have a fancy zip code. Even PTA races are about social climbing and networking. Baltimore isn't like that?"

"No. My parents are both ambitious, but it's not really about politics. My mom teaches at Johns Hopkins, my dad is a vice-president at an electronics company, and I'm the only one who even ended up in DC."

"But you *are* in DC. You didn't escape the vortex. It eats up everything around it."

"Not true. We even have our own baseball team. That's how you know it's a real city and not a suburb."

She snorted. "Tell that to the Los Angeles Angels of Anaheim."

I picked up a stick and pointed it at her like a sword. "I will duel for Baltimore's honor."

She grinned and pushed the stick aside. "If you love it so much, why don't you move there?" She said it in a schoolyard taunt voice, but I answered her seriously.

"I guess I feel needed in DC."

"I had you pegged for a cynic, not an idealist."

"Someone has to take out the trash."

"Is that what it feels like you're doing?"

I shrugged and sat on the fallen log she was peeling mushrooms from. "On a good day."

"And on a bad one?"

I sighed. "On a bad one, I remember coming to the capital for field trips in grade school and thinking we live in the best country on Earth. I wanted to be part of things. Work in the important buildings. Maybe work for the FBI catching bad guys. Or give important speeches or something. And it's depressing to realize there are so many of the bad guys. A lot of them pretending to be the good guys."

She gave a small smile. "I miss Capitol field trips. Wandering through the Smithsonian when you're a kid and being too dumb to appreciate the history but stoked to get out of school. I always liked that I got to buy lunch in the museum cafeteria, and I could spend the money on chips."

"Let me guess, your favorite was the natural history museum?"

"Bingo." She tilted her head to study me. "Yours was…the National Portrait Gallery?"

"For sure. Love me some boring paintings of old dead people."

She laughed, and I was glad to feel us slipping back into a comfortable groove. "Okay, what was your actual favorite? Air and Space?"

"That one was pretty cool, but mine's the International Spy Museum."

"Okay, James Bond."

"What do you mean, 'okay'?"

"I mean you made that up, or I would have heard of it."

"No, it's real," I said, laughing. "Google it. It opened when I was in high school."

She waved her hand, like, *Yeah, right.* "If it's not on Google, you owe me. You can pay up with coffee from Bixby's every morning next week."

"You got it. Too bad I won't be buying you any coffee."

She stared at me with a slightly more serious expression. "Spy museum, huh? I should have guessed that. So why not join the FBI or something?"

"I meant to," I confessed. I plucked at the bark on the log. "That's why I got my law degree. The FBI loves lawyers and accountants. But I guess I got impatient waiting for a chance to do my investigating, and I fell into it at the firm. And now…"

"Now?" she prompted, looking up from the mushroom she was examining when I didn't finish my thought.

But I wasn't going to, because how was I supposed to say, *Now I don't think they'd want me because I've had to skate an ethical line for so long that I'm not sure I haven't crossed it a few times.* I wasn't going to say that. I could barely make myself think it.

I pivoted. "And now it's time for you to tell me how field trips to

DC led an aspiring scientist to politics. Was it the field trips that planted the seed so that later you'd think, 'I can solve this with the law'? What was the arc?"

"It's partially that, yeah. They do a good job of making you think you can make a difference when you grow up."

"And you did. Why do you think you ended up in politics when a lot of us think the same thing and never do?"

"I'm driven, I guess. A problem-solver. I saw a problem in the vape regulations that cost me a friend, and I wanted to fix it."

"And you did."

"And I did." But she didn't smile like she was proud of it. "Being driven isn't great if you're going the wrong direction."

"How is it wrong if you did good in the world?" This was the piece I didn't understand about her story, and it made less sense to me the better I got to know her. She seemed like someone who would stay and fight, not run.

She caught her bottom lip between her teeth, and it made me want to do the same thing to it, lean over and kiss her. But I didn't want to be that guy who didn't listen, so I glanced up to her eyes instead. For a split second, I caught a flash of vulnerability in them that made me wonder if she would finally tell me the whole story of leaving DC. I wanted to be worthy of her secrets. Instead, she sighed. "There's more than one way to do good in the world. Despite Pantygate, this week has helped me feel more useful and optimistic than I have in a long time. The kids are good eggs." She stood and held out a hand to pull me to my feet.

Instead of letting go once I stood, I reached out to take her other hand too.

"Brooke," I said, when she kept her gaze on our clasped hands instead of meeting mine. Slowly, she looked up. The forest quieted, and all my senses tuned to her. The light smell of her shampoo tickled my nose over the earthy loam. My own heartbeat sounded loud in my ears. "You can talk to me. I want you to know that. But right this second, I've got something more on my mind than talking. If you're okay with that…"

I didn't even know what I would have said next, but it didn't matter because Brooke took a step toward me and rested her hand lightly against my chest. I didn't need any more permission than that, and I pulled her against me, finding her lips again, not sure if I was taking or giving a kiss this time. Brooke's body made me shiver with need everywhere we touched.

I'd kissed a lot of women, but none had been like this. The heat sprung up between us with the suddenness of a flame finding kindling. I explored her mouth as she threaded her fingers into my hair. I shuddered as it sent sparks down my nerve endings.

That seemed to break the spell, and she stepped back with a startled, "Oh."

I stared at her, now just out of arm's reach. "Oh." There was nothing else to say. For me, it was a word of understanding. I'd just found the woman meant to be in my arms. Why had she stepped away? "Are you okay?"

"Yeah, fine." But her hand fluttered to her hair to smooth it, though I hadn't kissed her long enough to mess it up. I should fix that. I reached for her again, but she took another step back, and I dropped my hand immediately.

"You sure?"

"I...yes. I'm good. But I should..." She waved toward the tote on the ground. "I think that's enough for my classes on Monday. I should get them home and prepped so they're ready for class."

"Brooke..."

"I really should get a hori hori," she said, with the forced brightness of chatter. "That's what real mushroom foragers use. It's a knife. For foraging. Mushrooms."

A wash of color crept into her cheeks. What should I do here? She was obviously distressed. Would it help more to address it? Or let it go until later? I decided to follow her lead. "There's a tool for everything, I guess."

"Well, not picking out the shells if you mess up cracking eggs."

"Fair enough. Invent it and make all the money."

"Nah." She settled her mesh bag into the tote and didn't protest when I took it from her to carry it myself. "Money is overrated."

Her bright tone had faded, and I wondered if she was thinking of whatever had earned her the settlement from Rink. I hated that I had summoned his shadow.

"I like money," I said, "but sure, call it names and hurt its feelings. See if it cares."

She rewarded me with a half-hearted smile, but it was something. "Race you to the car," she called, but the last part was over her shoulder as she stole a head start.

"Cheater," I said, taking off after her. I let her keep the lead until the last ten yards, then made sure we reached it in a tie.

"You let me win," she accused, grinning.

"No, I let you tie."

She gave me a light smack on the arm.

I caught her fingers, but before I could debate the wisdom of drawing her close again, she tugged them loose and darted around to the passenger side.

"Let me in, big bad wolf," she demanded.

I wiggled my eyebrows at her. "What does that make you? Goldilocks?"

She rolled her eyes. "That's bears. You need to take my biology class."

"Red Riding Hood?"

"Mmm, closer, but not quite. Snow White," she announced.

"There's no wolf in Snow White."

"Sure, there is." She tucked a stray hair behind her ear. "Remember how she charms all the animals? That's me and you. I charmed you even though you came back to Creekville thinking *you* were the one hunting a wolf. I tamed you."

I narrowed my eyes. "You better watch yourself. You're taking a hori hori to my fragile ego."

"Oh, your ego can withstand worse than a hori hori. It needs more like a chainsaw to cut it down."

"I'm offended."

"No, you aren't. Want to know why? Because I still haven't made a dent in your ego."

I grinned at her and disarmed the car alarm, rounding the car to open the door for her. "Don't make the mistake of thinking I don't bite," I murmured into her ear before she scrambled to safety inside.

CHAPTER TWENTY

Brooke

I acted as normally as I could on the drive home, answering Ian's questions about the high school and my house projects, but inside it was a pure freak out. *I just made out with Ian Greene in the woods.*

It was the most awesome bad idea I'd ever had.

But it was still such a bad, bad idea.

Ian insisted on dropping me off even though I told him he was being silly, and I could walk over from Miss Lily's.

"Would you like her to actually murder me?" he asked, turning into my driveway.

"I mean, I don't *not* want her to murder you."

"Ha. You'll get your wish if I don't use my best manners with you."

"If you get out of this car to open the door for me, I may find my hori hori."

"All right, all right," he muttered good-naturedly as I climbed out of the car. I waved as he backed out and drove the five seconds to Miss Lily's driveway, then let myself into the house, collapsing against the door.

"What in the actual hell just happened?" I said to the air. The remaining ugly wallpaper didn't answer. I stalked over and ripped off a strip.

"That was a very bad idea." I said it out loud, and hearing the words helped me believe them. "So bad. Dumb, dumb, dumb."

Another strip curled down and hung in front of my face like it was dangling an answer, nodding gently.

I laid out white paper on the kitchen counter and arranged the mushrooms on them to capture their spore patterns. When I had them all set out, I tackled the wallpaper again, but no matter how loud I turned the music or how hard I scraped at the old glue, my brain kept replaying that kiss on a loop. It had been…

Incredible.

The kind of thing that curled my toes in ways I'd thought romance writers only made up. But now I got it. Your toes curled because they were trying to hold onto the ground while the rest of you felt like it wanted to float away.

I'd made out with Ian Greene in the woods and had felt like I was leaving the earth.

This was so bad.

I chipped away at the wallpaper and glue for a couple more hours, but when lunch rolled around and Ian was still in every other thought, I decided I needed to take even more drastic action.

I pulled out my phone and texted him. *Meet me on my porch in 10 for a ham sandwich and a Coke?*

He sent me a thumbs up, and I threw together two ham sandwiches complete with thick slices of tomato from the garden.

Ten minutes later exactly, he knocked and I opened the door to hand him a plate with a sandwich and a cold Coke from the fridge.

"Go ahead and have a seat on the porch. Sorry I don't have furniture yet. I'll get to it eventually. Maybe even a swing. Pull up a stair, and I'll be out in a second."

I fetched my own lunch from the kitchen and sat beside him at the top of the steps, smiling when he bit into his sandwich and gave a happy sigh.

"Good sandwich," he said.

"Thank your grandmother for growing those tomatoes."

"I'll thank you too for helping her and for making the sandwich."

"Sure. It's the least I can do after your help today. You know, in the woods." I tried not to wince at how *not* smooth my lead-in was.

"The woods were great," he said, his tone carrying a faint question in it, like he knew I was getting at something.

"Right, so about that…" How was I supposed to say this?

"About the woods?" Now he sounded confused.

"Yeah. The woods. Or no. More like what happened *in* the woods." My cheeks flushed.

"Ah." The syllable was loaded with meaning. How did he put all those layers into a single sound?

"Right. So no more kissing." Wow. Could not have said that in a dumber-sounding way.

"No more kissing," he mused. "Why not? As a scientist, you should know I have a hypothesis that we might be really good at kissing each other."

"I'm not a scientist. I'm a science teacher."

"Right. And that was an excellent lesson in biology you gave me."

My cheeks straight up flamed. "It was not."

"You're right. More like chemistry."

I groaned. "How many versions are you going to do of that super lame joke?"

"Not a joke," he said even though a smile lurked at the corner of his lips. "More like an observation."

I rolled my eyes. "Fine. Then let's also have a geography lesson. About boundaries. And how I have them, and I'm not crossing them again. And my boundary with you is friendship. That side of the line is fine. Past it is not."

"So you're saying straight out you want me to stay in the friend zone?"

"Yes." *My brain does, anyway. The rest of me is not so sure about that.*

"Okay. I accept." He didn't even hesitate. "And trust me, I'm not the kind of guy who's going to try to talk you into anything different, but can I ask why? Just so I can understand."

"Because I'm not a casual dater," I said. "And we are way too different to ever work long-term, so I'd rather avoid a mess."

"A mess," he repeated. "You think I'm a mess?"

"No, I think dating you would be a mess."

"Why do you assume I want a long-term thing anyway?"

I stared down at my plate and pressed a crumb of bread to pick it up and nibble it off my finger. It wasn't that I wanted the crumb as much as I did *not* want to meet Ian's eyes. "I didn't mean to assume. But I don't have time to date at all right now, and if I did, I'm thinking long-term, so we're still not on the same page."

"It's a good thing you're not an English teacher, or you'd have to mark yourself down for all these clichés," he said, but his tone was teasing. "Friend zone, boundaries, same page."

"Happy to drop the subject. Just wanted to be clear."

"Okay. Except why do you think we'd be a mess?" He didn't sound annoyed, just curious, so I answered him.

"We want totally different things. You like your fast-paced life, the big city vibe, the whole environment. And I don't. I've had it, and I don't want it ever again. So what's the point of dating now when I'm sure we'd break up later?"

"Maybe you're a math teacher at heart, because that's a very calculating way to see it."

"If you make one more teaching pun, I'm going to find a hori hori."

He grinned. "Fine. I accept. On the condition that we are actually friends. Do I have to try and avoid you when I come to visit Gran from now on or do you mean it?"

"I mean it!" I gave it an overly enthusiastic emphasis that made him flinch. "I do. I'm all for being friends." *I mean it*, I told my heart again as it drooped at my words. *Behave.*

"Terms accepted. Your boundary is intact." He put his hands up. "See? Not coming anywhere near you."

"Thanks for understanding."

"Sure. Being friends with you isn't a consolation prize. I like you as a person, and eventually I'll get over the urge to kiss you stupid."

I'd just taken a sip of my Coke when he laid that on me. He smiled at me blandly while I choked.

"You okay there?"

"Fine," I wheezed and coughed again to clear my throat. "Why do I feel like you're not taking this new friendship very seriously?"

"I was teasing. I promise I mean it. You're worth knowing. I'd like to be able to talk or eat ham sandwiches or hunt mushrooms with you any time I drop in to see Gran for a weekend."

I nodded, not trusting myself not to say the exact wrong thing again. We finished our sandwiches in silence, and though it felt awkward at first, it became comfortable by the time I swallowed the last delicious bite.

"So as your friend, I'm curious what the prospects are like in Creekville," he said when his sandwich was gone. "Is there a happening dating scene around here?"

I thought about Noah for a second. "Not really? I don't know. I haven't been looking for one, but I sort of get the impression that Miss Lily would be lining me up with church boys if she didn't have you to marry off, and I think the secretary at school is looking for an opening to set me up with a nephew she keeps bringing up."

"Sounds grim," he said.

"More grim than dating apps and pub crawls?"

"Good point."

"What's your DC dating life like? When I worked there, it was hard to find time. People mostly seemed to hang out with people from their office or offices nearby. Not a lot of time for one-on-one, traditional dates."

He shrugged. "I'm a little old school. I like dating the old-fashioned way, I guess. Set a time and place, pick up my date, spend time getting to know each other over a good meal. But I tend to always date the same kind of woman."

"What's your type?" Was I some kind of sadist? But I really wanted to know. It was the kind of thing I'd ask any of my other friends.

"I don't have a physical type, I guess. But I do date a lot of lawyers."

"Like from your firm?"

"Some," he acknowledged.

"You don't worry they're all going to get together and compare notes and you're going to be in hot water?"

He shook his head. "No. I was brought up to be a gentleman. I don't date more than one woman from our firm at a time, and we always leave on good terms. I guess it's possible they get together and trash me, but I kind of feel like I maintain a good working relationship with all of them? I never hide anything from them, and I try to communicate well."

I stared at him. "Are you the actual perfect man?"

He snorted. "Obviously not or we'd be making out right now."

"Ian..." My cheeks heated for the fiftieth time.

"I kid, I kid. No, I'm not the perfect guy. I'm a workaholic. I tend to put it before anything else. I tease too much. And I don't visit my grandmother enough," he added.

"That's true. You've done better coming to see her the last couple weekends," I conceded.

"I forget sometimes how much I love being here. Her trick did a good job of getting me back here to remind me of that."

"Even breathing the air here feels like therapy." I inhaled deeply and picked up notes of garden soil, the faint whiff of freshly cut grass from a neighbor's yard, and a freshness that I couldn't describe but that was the essence of Creekville.

"Very true. Almost as good as Gran's hugs. Speaking of which, I better get back to her. I promised I'd play cards with her and Mary. I'm sure they'd love it if you joined us. You should know that Gran cheats like a senator."

Spending the afternoon playing cards and laughing with them sounded perfect, but I needed to reinforce our new friendship boundary with some time and distance. And honestly, I probably needed the reinforcement more than he did as he rose from the porch and stretched for a minute, the hem of his shirt creeping up enough to let me peek at his washboard abs.

I glanced over at Miss Lily's house to distract myself. "Thanks, but

I'm going to spend some time prepping fungi for class on Monday. Try not to be jealous of my exciting life."

"Then I'll head back. See you around, Brooke Spencer."

"See you around, Ian Greene."

I watched him walk away. That had gone exactly like I wanted it to. So why did it feel like I was missing out?

CHAPTER TWENTY-ONE

Ian

Brooke's "just friends" talk made perfect sense. It was also easier said than done. I drove back to DC Sunday night, trying to focus on the Rink case, but thoughts of Brooke slipped in the whole way home. It would always start with wondering how she'd been affected by the predatory senator. It always ended with me thinking about the places I'd like to take her to in DC. Or what we'd do the next weekend at Gran's. Or making out with her again.

How come stripping wallpaper and hunting mushrooms with her was more entertaining than swanky dinners with gorgeous women?

In the office Monday, Sherrie dropped in to report on her incredibly productive weekend. It was a good distraction from Brooke, and by the time Sherrie was done detailing how she'd met with one of Rink's victims, I realized we had so much work ahead of us following down leads that I'd easily be working through the upcoming weekend.

It was for the best. I needed a week or two to get Brooke out of my system before I went out to visit Gran again.

By Thursday, Brooke was still on my mind. A lot. More than other "friends" had ever been on my mind. I hadn't been so fixated on a girl since high school. I was tempted to drive out to Gran's tomorrow anyway, but it would only make it worse.

Instead, I called a woman I'd met at an embassy party a few weeks before. What was her name? Charlotte. She was a human rights attorney working on building a case against a small Asian country I'd barely heard of.

She agreed to dinner for Friday night, and when I picked her up, she was as attractive as I remembered. She was smart and funny, though her humor had a bite to it as she pilloried the opposing counsel on her case. But as interesting as her work was, I found my mind wandering.

What was Brooke up to? Were she and Gran having dinner? Had Mary made roast again? Because her roast still beat the thirty-dollar steak I was eating.

After I had to force my focus back to Charlotte for the fifth time, I made a mental note: stay away from Creekville and Brooke for at least another week.

I wouldn't be *that* guy, the one who thought he knew better than a woman did what she needed for herself. Brooke seemed very sure of who she was and what she needed. Until I could show up well and truly as her friend and *only* her friend, I'd stay away a little longer.

It helped that the Rink case kept me busy through the weekend. Sherrie's source had worked in the senator's office five years previously—before Brooke had gotten there—and while she said the senator didn't do anything that bordered on assault, he'd definitely veered into harassment. She didn't want to come forward without anything more than comments he made that could be twisted to look innocent, but she'd provided names of other employees past and present who she'd heard through the whisper network might have bigger grievances.

Tracking them down and combing through their social media was enough to keep me from getting in the car and driving out to Gran's. The diversion felt like it was working until Gran's name flashed in my phone on Sunday afternoon.

"Ian-boy, why didn't you come see me this weekend?"

"I told you, Gran. I'm slammed at work."

"I have Wi-Fi, you know. You can work from here and at least I'd see you some instead of none."

"Ah, Gran, you know I want to. But to be honest, I'm trying to stay out of Brooke's way a little bit too."

"Why? You should be in that girl's way as much as possible. She's good for you."

"Maybe, but she only wants to be friends."

Gran scoffed. "She most certainly does not."

"I ate lunch on her porch last weekend, and her exact words were, 'Let's just be friends.' I have to respect that."

I listened while Gran muttered a bit, but she'd covered up the receiver, so I couldn't be sure what she said. Must be some cussing in there or she would have said it straight to me.

"Gran?" I prodded when she fell silent.

"Who knew *she'd* be the hard one in this equation?" she grumbled.

"Leave her alone, Gran. I'm respecting her wishes. You're supposed to tell me what a good boy I am."

"You *are* a good boy, but Brooke could use a spanking."

"She's fine. I'll get over it. I even went on a date Friday." It was a strategic error to bring it up. I'd meant to distract her. Instead, Gran dug in.

"How'd it go?"

"Fine. Good dinner, good company."

"Don't lie to Gran."

"I'm not. She was a nice lady with lots of interesting things to say."

"You were bored." Gran's voice held such a note of certainty that I couldn't deny it.

"How do you know?"

"Ian, how many times do I have to tell you: if you always do what you always did, you'll always get what you've always got. And you always date the same kind of woman."

"There's nothing wrong with the women I date."

"Except that they're all in DC. I know you like women with strong personalities to stand up to you and busy careers so they understand your devotion to yours. Am I wrong?"

"No. But there's nothing wrong with a strong-willed career woman."

"Nothing wrong at all," she agreed. "And that's exactly what Brooke is and why I picked her for you. She was just smart enough to leave DC before the city started eating her up. She throws herself into her work here as much as anyone you're going to date in that town. That place is giving you a hard crust, Ian. It's not good for you. It would be different if you were spending time with the good people there. But you're always dealing with the rats and weasels."

She wasn't wrong. There was no point in arguing, but I tried. "I like Brooke, but I'm not what Brooke wants. Give me a couple of weeks to get her out of my system before I come back around."

"Fools, the both of you," she declared. "Neither of you knows what you need."

"Can I just get a gold star for respecting her wishes?"

More grumbling. "Fine. But stop dating lawyers."

I decided to ignore Gran's advice and went out with a couple more lawyers in the next two weeks in between working on the Rink case. They were both attractive, smart, and ultimately like every other woman I'd dated since graduating from law school. Both dates only made me think of how easy it was to hang out with Brooke.

Luckily, work kept me too busy to dwell on it much. We were *so close* with the Rink case. All we needed was a witness willing to go on record about her experiences with him. If we got one, another would follow. But all of them were either bound by non-disclosure agreements or too worried about the senator's reach to come forward.

"Keep looking," I ordered Sherrie after our fifth victim declined to go public. "There are more out there, and one of them will eventually help us take this guy down."

"You got it, boss," she said, rising from her seat. "Hey, not to overstep, but I have a niece coming into town who I think you'd like. What do you think about me bringing her by to meet you? Maybe you guys could grab lunch or something."

"Sure, that sounds great. Just promise not to quit on me if we don't hit it off."

"Never, boss. I'll bring her by Friday. She's a cutie. Look," she said, pulling up a photo to show me. Her niece was a striking brunette with dark eyes and bold red lipstick.

"Cutie is underselling it. But can she carry on a conversation?"

"Top of her class at the Kennedy Institute," she said proudly.

"Thanks for thinking I'm a decent enough guy to introduce her to."

Sherrie rolled her eyes and pointed at me. "Saying stuff like that is exactly what makes you a decent guy. You'll love her."

"I look forward to it," I said. She left my office with a wave, but despite meaning every word I said to her, I found myself clicking away from a picture of Rink's weekend home to do a search on porch swings instead, because somehow, imagining Brooke having one of her own and spending a lazy Sunday afternoon in it had become the calm I needed in the never-ending capital rat race.

CHAPTER TWENTY-TWO

Brooke

Week two of school went better, mainly because I wore pants every day just to make sure I didn't tuck my skirt into my underwear again. It was a low bar, sure, but I needed an uneventful week after the first one from hell.

As a bonus, the microscope activity went well, and the kids loved doing an actual lab. It bought me some goodwill for the rest of the week. I tried not to worry about how I would top it the next week, and just enjoyed having everything work well. By Friday afternoon, I even managed to settle one rambunctious boy with a single look. The Look. The *teacher* look.

I couldn't wait to tell Miss Lily about it after school while we worked in the garden.

"You got *the look* down on your second week of school?" she repeated. "Impressive, but I'm not surprised. You're a fast learner."

"It doesn't feel like that," I confessed. "I feel like they're going to see right through me every single day, like my days are numbered before they figure out I'm not a real teacher."

"Keep thinking that and they will, honey." She leaned over from where she was weeding eggplants next to me and patted my hand. "Just remember, you may be an inexperienced teacher, but you're an experienced human. You've lived twice as much life as they have, and that counts for something. Let your authority rest in that, and pretty soon they'll believe you're a regular old teacher like everyone else over there."

"I hope so." I rose to stretch my back before I tackled the next row. And to steal a glance at the road.

"You looking for Ian?"

"No." I crouched down and went to work on the row on the other side.

Miss Lily continued like she hadn't heard my denial. "Don't know if he's coming this weekend, to be honest. Says he's got work. And probably another date."

Another date? A-n-o-t-h-e-r.

I wanted to follow up on that except I'd gone out of my way to make sure it was none of my business.

"Don't worry, honey. He'll see sense eventually. He always does."

"What do you mean?"

"He'll realize it's you he should be taking out."

"Oh, that's not what I—"

"Yes, it is." She was probably trying to save me from telling a lie.

But I didn't want her feeling sorry for me, so some stubborn part of me lied anyway. "I wasn't thinking about Ian, Miss Lily. In fact, I have a date tonight."

Miss Lily scooted around so she faced me again. "Come again?"

"I have a date tonight." The lie tasted worse the second time.

"With who?" She said it like she didn't believe me which made me feel like I needed to double down on the lie.

"Noah Redmond?"

"Is that a question?"

"No, I mean, I'm going to dinner with Noah Redmond."

"The new PE teacher." She seemed to consider this. "All right. I hear his people are good. They're over in Lynchburg."

"Right. We eat lunch together most days, and he's nice. Helps to not be the only new face on staff."

"Tell me about your classes," she said, turning back to her weeding, and I did, not sure how I felt about her giving up on the idea of me dating Ian so easily. It was for the best, of course. It was a good thing she wasn't too worked up over it. I didn't like disappointing her.

But...there had been something so nice about her having a high enough opinion of me that she'd lured her grandson home to meet me in the first place.

After an hour of chatting and weeding, I stood and held out a hand to help her to her feet. "I should head in. I need to get ready." *For the date I made up.*

Miss Lily accepted my hand and rose. "Well, you have a good time, honey. I'll see you out here tomorrow, and we'll plant some of that trendy kale and then some actual good lettuces."

"Can I take a couple of ears of corn?" The first stalks were ripening, and we had two whole rows of it growing.

"Are you crazy, child? Of course not."

I looked at her, startled by her denial.

"Unless you can pluck it and eat it fresh, leave it on the stalk. It loses most of its sugar within two hours of being plucked. Trust me, you're going to want to eat it tomorrow when you're not rushing off to dinner with someone who is a poor second place to my grandson." Then she winked and strode off toward her house with the energy of a woman half her age.

I let myself into my kitchen, smiling, because it was reassuring that Miss Lily still wanted me for Ian. But then I felt like trash for lying to her about Noah, so I decided to cowgirl up and try to make it the truth.

He'd offered his number in case I ever needed help with spider-wrangling, and we often texted to confirm lunch plans before he made the trek across campus. I had so far declined the opportunity to eat lunch in the stinky gym. I thought for a minute and drafted a text to Noah.

Hey, so feeling like I want to try a place in town but don't want to be a loser at a table by myself tonight. You up for dinner?

I read it over, decided it sounded non-datey, and pressed send.

Noah answered a couple minutes later. *Don't know. I had my eye on a Lean Cuisine.*

I laughed. *You're right. Gourmet burgers can't compete.*

He responded immediately. *Lit the Lean Cuisine on fire and threw it in the trash. What time for dinner?*

I suggested meeting at the Three Penny Pub at 7:00, and he confirmed he'd be there.

Who knew? Maybe we'd find a vibe with each other that didn't necessarily show up at work?

I came home shortly after nine, full and sleepy after a fun night at the pub with Noah, but it hadn't felt remotely date-like. Fun and easy, yes. Romantic? No.

And annoyingly, I'd found myself checking Miss Lily's driveway for a BMW and frowning when I didn't see it.

Maybe that was why when Noah suggested dinner out at an Italian place the following week, I said yes. This time, he offered to come pick me up. That was more date-ish. I even put on a dress for it.

But from the minute he knocked on my door, I knew we were as friend-zoned as I'd tried to pretend Ian and I were.

In fact, something about Noah coming to my house turned us both awkward. Where conversation usually flowed easily between us at school, we kept falling into pockets of silence in the car, and by the time our orders arrived, I was beginning to wonder if I'd ever known how to carry on a conversation.

I poked at my ravioli. I didn't even want it, but my mom had always taught me not to order noodles on a date because there was no elegant way to eat them. I shot a covetous look at Noah's plate of fettucine alfredo, wishing I'd ordered that instead.

"Something wrong with the food?" Noah asked.

"No, it's fine." I took a bite. "Yum. Good marinara."

He nodded and swirled some noodles onto his fork. "Good alfredo."

We ate in silence for a couple of minutes, but the awkwardness made it feel like two hours.

"So what—"

"Is it me—"

He laughed. "It figures we'd both try to break the silence at the same time."

I smiled back. "You go ahead. What were you going to say?"

"I'm wondering if it's me or this whole evening has felt weird to you so far?"

"Super weird," I confessed.

"Is it because we tried to treat it like a date? Wait," he said, holding up his hands. "Don't answer that. Of course it is. Sorry. I think I made it weird by coming to pick you up."

"I made it weird by wearing a dress to dinner."

He nodded. "You could always tuck it into your underwear. Bring things back to normal."

I grinned. "I actually think that would make me feel better. But I'm not doing it."

"Fair enough. So how do we reset?"

"How about if we call this not a date? And I pay for my own dinner and confess that I wish I had gotten the fettucine. I only got the ravioli because I thought I could eat it more neatly on a date than noodles."

His face lit up. "I didn't get the ravioli because I figured I'd probably drop some on my shirt and end up with a marinara stain. Want to trade? And never go on a date with each other again?"

"Heck, yes!" I said and held out my plate for the swap.

"So much better," he said after his first bite of ravioli.

"No way. I came out better in that trade," I answered after trying the fettucine. "Tastes even better when it's seasoned with friendship."

He held up his wine glass for a toast and I obliged. "To never trying *that* again."

"Cheers!"

Dinner went much better from there as we settled into our usual rhythm of jokes and school gossip. He dropped me off and I slipped in the house, grateful that we'd worked things out but frustrated that my eyes had searched for Ian's car once again the second Miss Lily's house was in view.

Ugh.

Get your mind right, Brooke. He's a bad fit. Move on.

Which would have been far easier to do if a delivery man hadn't rung my doorbell mid-morning the next day with a huge cardboard box.

"What is it?" I asked when I opened the door to the delivery guy.

"No idea," he said. "Heavy sucker though."

"Who's it from?"

"Don't know that either. Try the mailing sticker."

"Thanks, I would have never thought of that," I muttered as he jogged down the stairs.

He'd propped the box beside the front door, and it was as tall as I was. It was also very solid when I nudged it with my toe. He'd faced the shipping label inward, so I had to wrestle it around before I could find the sender. All it said was Virginia Woodcraft.

I wracked my brain trying to think of what I could have ordered from them, but I didn't remember buying anything online lately, and definitely nothing this size. The only thing left to do was open it. I fetched a pocketknife inside, carefully eased the box flat on the porch, and sliced through the tape.

When I pulled away the cardboard, it looked like a wooden bench made of white-painted wood along with two packages of sturdy chains.

A porch swing? "What in the world..." I dug through the packaging again, but there were no further clues to be had.

Who would send me a porch swing?

I had only ever mentioned the idea to...

Ian.

As if I'd summoned him, my phone vibrated with a text, and his name appeared in my screen. It had been a couple of weeks since I'd heard from him, and my heart did a dopey skipped beat as I opened the message.

Got a delivery alert. Finally figured out how to say sorry like I really mean it. You deserve a porch swing. Let me know when you want it installed and I'll send Grace over to do it.

I had the strangest feeling of my heart leaping while my stomach sank.

He listened to me!

He sent me a porch swing!

He would hire someone else to hang it rather than come do it himself...

"Brooke Spencer, you are a ridiculous person." But saying it out loud didn't make me feel any less simultaneously goofy and annoyed as I picked up and admired each piece of the swing.

I should say no to this, I finally texted back. *But I love it too much. So thank you.*

There was a long pause before he responded. *It was the least I could do.*

I closed the box and pushed it against the far edge of the porch until I could get to it, then went inside to get the remaining wallpaper down. But as I worked by myself removing the last pieces from the entryway, instead of the sense of satisfaction that the unending project had an end after all, I pulled the final piece away and realized that I missed listening to Ian do it while he muttered curses to himself when he thought I wasn't listening.

I missed Ian, period.

The failed date with Noah last night only highlighted what I'd been trying to deny to myself: I was into Ian. In a big way. In a one-slight-nudge-and-I'll-fall-madly kind of way. And while I hadn't tumbled yet, he was going to be the shadow looming over any other dates I might have a chance to go on, now or six months from now.

I sat down hard, right in the middle of the foyer amidst the curls of old wallpaper.

What the heck was I supposed to do about that?

I tried to think through all the possibilities.

I could throw myself into my work! But that hadn't helped take my mind off him so far.

I could try a dating app! But the nearest candidates were an hour away in Charlottesville, and none of their pictures showed the same glint in their eyes that Ian had.

I could ask Miss Lily to set me up with a nice church boy! But I liked Ian's devilish streak.

I just really liked Ian.

Finally, I pushed up from the floor, dragged myself into the kitchen and fixed myself a cup of fortifying tea before I made my next call. I bowed my head in defeat and surrendered to the inevitable.

"Hey, Mom? I was thinking about coming to visit next weekend over Labor Day."

CHAPTER TWENTY-THREE

Ian

The Rink case was killing me. Or making me want to murder something. I tried to take out my frustration in the batting cages with Landon after work one evening, but even smashing the pitches from the machine didn't make me feel any better.

"Yo, Ian, you good?" My brother looked at me with concerned eyes from beneath the bill of his Orioles cap.

"Fine." I smashed another pitch and grunted.

"You sound real fine," he said, his lips twisting.

"It's just a case. I keep turning up leads and they keep running into dead ends."

"At least you don't have to do the paperwork on it."

I stepped out of the strike zone to study him more closely. "You getting tired of your job? About time. It only took me a year." He was a second-year associate at the largest firm in Baltimore.

"I'm tired of grunt work."

"It's the nature of the beast, man. You gotta put in time before you get to do the interesting stuff."

"You didn't."

I grinned at him. "No, I sure didn't. I jumped right to the interesting part."

"But you'll never see the inside of a courtroom."

I shrugged. "Overrated. I like being where the action is, doing the research, solving puzzles. It's a good fit for me."

"Then why are you so frustrated that you dragged me to the batting cages tonight?"

I gave him a tight smile this time and kicked at my bat. "Because the puzzle isn't solving. Or maybe the better way to say it is that I know exactly what this puzzle is but I'm missing the last piece."

"Can't find it?"

"Yes and no."

"Talk to me in hypotheticals."

I thought about how to say it in a way that kept me inside the right ethical lines. "Imagine you have a big, powerful guy named Bad Guy."

"Creative."

"Shut up. I didn't go to novel-writing school. So Bad Guy has a history of doing bad things to nice women."

"How bad?"

"Not exactly sure, but bad enough that he's had to pay several of them a lot of money to stay quiet. And let's say that Bad Guy has fooled the world into thinking he's reformed, but I know he hasn't. And let's say that Bad Guy has a lot of influence that he doesn't deserve, and worse, constant access to new victims. So Bad Guy needs to go down."

Landon thumped his bat in his open palm, like a goon in a mafia movie threatening a small-time crook. "Yeah, he does."

"Yeah. He really does. So, we need one of his victims to come forward. And if one comes forward, more will come forward. But none of them want to cross him because they think he'll retaliate. Or that the system won't believe them."

"You can't find any of his victims?"

I frowned. "Worse. I can find plenty. But all of them are afraid to take the first step." I'd spent more than two weeks tracking down leads. I'd talked to six young women, and Sherrie had spoken with another four. Even the ones who didn't have non-disclosure agreements didn't want to come forward. Rink's influence was that great.

"Can you blame them?" he asked. "It doesn't always go well for women who speak up."

I sighed. "I know. But the reality is that he's going to keep preying on new women because he knows he can. It kills me."

He nodded and stepped into the strike zone, squaring up. "So you keep looking until you find someone who will."

"It's not that simple."

"I know you're the older, wiser brother, but it's exactly that simple. It's also very hard. But you have to do it." He swung and connected with the next pitch, the crack of the bat underlining his point.

"I know."

"That everything?" he asked.

"Sure."

"Liar. Gran says there's a girl."

I rolled my eyes. "There's no girl. She tried to trick me into dating her neighbor."

"Something wrong with the neighbor?"

"No, she's great. Just not looking to date."

"She isn't or you aren't?"

"She isn't—" But I lost my train of thought as my watch vibrated with a text from Brooke. I hadn't heard from her since last week when I'd sent the porch swing.

Heading to McLean to see my parents tmrw. Thought I'd check out the spy museum you made up. You free to prove it's real?

I smiled.

"Whoa, what's that smile?" Landon asked. "It can only mean a woman."

"The neighbor, actually."

"The one who doesn't want to date?"

"The very one."

"What's the text say? Did she change her mind?"

KISS ME NOW

I re-read the message. "I can't tell. She friend-zoned me, but now she's asking if I want to go to a museum Saturday."

"Like a date?"

I thought back to our last conversation. "I don't think so. She's pretty stubborn. I think she means as friends."

"And this is a chick you want to be friends with and go hang out with in museums?"

I was quiet long enough that he stepped out of the strike zone to watch me more closely and let the next pitch pass.

"You like her," he said.

"I did."

"Go to the museum Saturday."

But I was already shaking my head. "Bad idea. I need more distance before I can honestly say I'd be there as her friend."

"You got moves. You could change her mind."

I gave him my best big brother "knock it off" stare. "No, dummy. It's not a game. I'm listening and respecting her because that's what good guys do."

He scoffed. "Sure. Good guys who don't want to date their gran's hot neighbors. But you do want to date her."

"Maybe me from a few months ago would have agreed with you. But after looking into Ri—uh, Bad Guy, pushing the issue is what he would do. And I won't be like that."

"Fair enough." He seemed to lose interest as he focused on the incoming pitches, hitting more than he missed.

I kept reading over Brooke's message, trying hard to figure out how to respond. I knew what I wanted to say. But I finally texted back what I knew I *should* say. *Wish I could but slammed with work. Have a good time.*

Her reply came several minutes later. *Will save it for another time with you. Think I'll spend the morning with Willard instead.*

Willard? Who? I texted back.

The mega-toothed shark exhibit at the Natural History Museum. I have a thing for him.

I snorted. *Sounds dead sexy.*

Well, dead anyway, she texted back, and that made me laugh out loud. I sent her a gif of Jaws chomping on the back of the boat.

Landon and I each went home for the night, but the next day, Friday, the closer it got to school letting out, the more my mind drifted to Brooke. Was she on the road out to her parents' place yet? Or would she wait out traffic? Although…she'd be going against it, so maybe she was on her way now, leaving right after school to make it by dinner.

I could call her, take her up on her museum offer the next day. I'd love to spend time revisiting the good parts of DC with her, the parts I often forgot about with the frustrations of my job.

But no. I didn't think I could hang out with her in the just friends capacity. I still needed time for my brain to switch gears.

Saturday morning, I went into the office to keep myself busy around the time I figured she'd be hitting the museum. It wasn't that unusual to see people in the office on the weekend, but I was still surprised to find Sherrie at her desk outside my office.

"What are you doing here?" I asked. "Don't you have kid soccer games to go harass the other parents at?"

"Not until this afternoon. Wanted to pull on a thread in the Rink case without my kids in my hair."

My eyebrows went up. "Anything good?"

"Maybe. I'll keep you posted."

I settled into my office and spent some time trying to investigate financials to eliminate any possible witnesses who had received a settlement from the senator. They'd be bound by NDAs and less likely to come forward.

My attention kept wandering to my phone, wondering where Brooke was now. It hadn't been too hard to talk myself into staying in town to keep my distance the last couple of weekends; I used all my usual workaholic excuses. But it was totally different knowing she was *right here*, right in the capital, maybe even a few blocks away somewhere in the maze of the Smithsonian.

After an hour, I couldn't resist anymore. I reached for my phone and checked her Instagram. She posted about once a day, usually tailoring her posts for her students as she documented interesting stuff in the garden or from exploring the countryside around Creekville.

Bingo. She'd posted ten minutes before but from the National Zoo, her face beaming in delight as she took a selfie with the panda exhibit in the background. The caption said, "Life under the microscope is cool, but studying biology is even better in person!"

Man, I loved that smile.

Well, not *loved*. Not like that. But I'd really missed seeing it.

I made a decision that I decided not to second guess. "I'm going out for lunch," I told Sherrie. "Will you be here later?"

"For a couple more hours, at least. Eat something good."

"You want anything?"

"Caesar salad with chicken, thanks."

The zoo wasn't far, but I didn't want to waste time by walking, so I drove over, parked, and walked in. Like all Smithsonian exhibits, the zoo was free, but I hesitated at the entrance, studying the map to guess where she might be. It had been almost a half hour since Brooke had posted from the panda exhibit. She could be anywhere in the zoo right now if she hadn't left.

Apes. I couldn't say why, but a gut feeling said she'd be there.

I took the shortest route, and sure enough, as soon as I walked through the arch into the Great Ape House, I spotted the blue shirt Brooke had been wearing in her post. She stood watching an enormous silverback female grooming a baby gorilla. I was sort of indifferent to animals, but even I smiled at the cuteness of the ugly little thing.

I got close enough to be heard over the other zoo visitors but not close enough to scare her. "I have a theory that the uglier a baby is, the cuter it is."

Brooke jumped and turned. "Ian!"

"Hey." I tried not to grin like an idiot, but the corners of my mouth weren't cooperating. Dang, I had missed her.

"What are you doing here?" she demanded even as she came over to hug me.

Maybe she meant it to be a quick and friendly hello, but it lasted longer than the hugs I gave any of my friends. I couldn't tell if it was her or me.

"I wanted to see some apes," I said when she stepped back after a minute.

"How did you find me?"

"Did you forget what I do for a living?"

She stepped back and gave me a slight smile. "You followed my Instagram."

"Was hoping for some sexy Willard content."

Her smile got bigger. "Want to go see the pandas again? They mostly sleep but they're still so cute."

"Sure."

She reached out like she was going to take my arm but then dropped her hands to her sides. "Let's go. How's life?"

"Boring," I reported as we headed to the pandas. "All work, all the time."

"Same."

"Tell me about the house. How's the makeover going?"

She kept me entertained with her list of grievances and triumphs as we walked over. The house became a character the way she talked about it, and it made me want to show up the next weekend to dig in and help her with the work.

"Thanks again for the swing," she said as we lined up to see the pandas. "I'm waiting to put it up as a reward for finishing all the downstairs walls. Thinking about sitting in it in the evenings is getting me through some long hours of spackling and sanding."

"It's good you took a break." I wanted her to say she'd driven out because she missed me. I knew she wouldn't. But it didn't change the wanting.

She shrugged. "I decided to celebrate Labor Day weekend by not laboring."

"Fair enough."

We admired the pandas for a while, and when we had to move on or risk antagonizing the people waiting behind us, we left the exhibit and wandered the path that led toward the park entrance.

"Thanks for taking a break from work with me," she said.

"Sure. Guess I should probably head back to the office." Not because the work *had* to get done, but because I could feel Brooke drawing me in. Not that she was trying. It was more honest to say I felt myself being drawn to her again. It made the friend zone boundaries blurry.

"Right." She was quiet for a moment, and it was the first silence to fall between us. It was awkward. Like talking-to-your-boss's-wife awkward.

"Do you want to get some lunch? We could grab something and eat it at my desk. Not the most exciting offer, but I do know some good places."

"All food sounds exciting when you're starving. That sounds great."

I led her to my car and drove the short distance to a sandwich shop that I knew would have Sherrie's salad, then drove back to the firm.

As I waved my badge to unlock the front entrance, I wondered how Fleming, Roth, and Schill would look through her eyes. The building was eight stories of glass and chrome with an interior of marble, granite, and wood. Our firm occupied the top three floors, and as we left the elevator, we stepped into the more traditional trappings of law offices: rich mahogany furniture, expensive sculptures on tasteful tables, plush seats in the reception area, beige walls, and burgundy carpets.

I led her through reception into the warren of desks and toward my small office. Normally only partners got offices—and theirs were at least twice the size of my glorified closet—but some of my work required discretion, and an open desk wouldn't cut it.

"It looks like my assistant stepped out," I said as we passed Sherrie's empty desk. I set her salad down.

"Should you refrigerate it?" Brooke asked. "The biology teacher in me freaks out a little about food safety."

"Nah. She's close by."

"How do you know?"

"It hurts my feelings that you think I suck at my job." I nodded toward Sherrie's purse, tucked beneath her desk but still visible.

"Ah, right. Sorry, Sherlock."

I led her into my office and set our food on the desk. She took the client side and started unpacking the bag, an Italian sub for me and a club sandwich for her.

"I thought you liked tomatoes," I said as she unwrapped the sandwich she'd requested to be tomato-free.

"I do. But Miss Lily's spoiled me, and now I can't stand any that don't come straight off the vine."

"I see. High maintenance. Got it."

She rolled her eyes. "Yeah. So high maintenance with my ponytail and overalls couture, and my constant need to be in the dirt."

I grinned. "Gran has that effect on people."

"She makes them want to be in the dirt?"

"In the garden, anyway."

"And yet you stayed away for a long time. And you're staying away again."

I thought about what I should say here, because Brooke was the reason I was staying away. Telling the truth seemed like another way of pushing on her friend zone boundary, so I shrugged and let it drop. I took a bite of my sandwich to get out of answering.

Brooke took the hint and changed the subject. "Working on anything interesting right now?"

Worst possible subject change. *Yeah. The case most likely to upset you.* "Uh, couple of big things but kind of boring."

"I used to find all of this interesting. Maybe I will again. Try me."

I cleared my throat, trying to figure out what to say, when the office door flew open, and Sherrie barreled in.

"We got him! We got Rink cold!" She was staring down at a file in her hands, but when she looked up, grinning, and spotted Brooke, her smile froze. "Oh, hey. Sorry, Ian. Didn't know you had company."

"Sherrie, this is Brooke Spencer." Sherrie's face didn't change expression to give away that she knew who Brooke was. Good. Sherrie was getting better all the time. "Brooke, this is my assistant, Sherrie."

"Nice to meet you," Sherrie said.

But Brooke ignored that. "Rink?"

"Oh, that's just business. A case," Sherrie said, waving her hand like she could swat away his name.

"Senator Rink?" Brooke's voice had gone tight and quiet, and she looked pale. She turned to me. "You're investigating Senator Rink?"

Sherrie and I exchanged glances. We *could* tell Brooke since Rink wasn't our client, but that didn't mean we should. Not unless she wanted to help bring him down. I quickly catalogued what I knew about her so far. She had an NDA with Rink, and she couldn't speak about him without nullifying her settlement. But she also had a strong sense of right and wrong that might make her anxious to help.

"Yeah, we're investigating him," I said quietly.

"I'm going to go eat my lunch before it gets...uh, I'm going to go eat." Sherrie stepped out and closed the door behind her.

"How much do you know?" Brooke asked.

I hesitated again, unsure how to navigate this.

"How much?" she repeated.

"More than you would want to tell me," I acknowledged.

"Did you bring me here to try to get more dirt on him?"

"Brooke, no." I leaned toward her across the desk. "Of course not. I didn't even know you were going to be in town until a couple of days ago."

"So? How would that stop you from charming me into your office?"

"I swear to you, until I got up and walked out the door to find you in the zoo, I had no idea I was going to do it."

"Right. Well." She folded the paper around her barely eaten sandwich. "Thanks for lunch, but I lost my appetite. Think I might go back to the zoo and check out the snake house."

I winced. "Brooke, that's not—"

"It's fine, Ian." She rose, hitched her purse over her shoulder, her hand on the door before I could even round the desk.

"Brooke, wait. Hear me out." She paused, not pulling the door open yet. "I don't know what Rink did to you, but I'm dead sure he was guilty of something. Probably something bad." A brief flicker of pain crossed her face. "We've got a shot of bringing him down. If I had to guess, Sherrie was coming in to tell me that she's found a victim to come out publicly against him."

Brooke flinched at the word "victim." It was so slight, but I was watching her too closely to miss it, and I hated thinking of her in that context. "We've been looking for someone willing to speak out against him, and we're hoping that once the first woman comes forward, it will give other women the courage to do the same thing."

Her face hardened. "So if I don't want to speak out against him, it's because I'm a coward?"

"No! No, of course not. It's smart. It's self-preservation. But the risk to you—to any of you—goes down with every witness who comes forward. This is the beginning of the end for him, Brooke. You can be part of that." I'd heard enough from the women we'd found to make me sick to my stomach, to make me angry enough to yank the senator from his expensive Mercedes and pound him to a pulp in the driveway of his townhouse, maybe with Landon and his baseball bat to make sure he got the message.

"You will never know what he cost me." Her voice was cold but her eyes blazed. "But I rebuilt myself out of ashes. How dare you ask me to light myself on fire again? I'm done, Ian. I'll see myself out."

"Brooke, let me—"

"No. Stop. I'm going to walk back to the zoo, pick up my car, and drive home. All the way home. I'll see myself out."

I followed her out of the office then stood helplessly and watched her leave. I knew if I tried to say anything, it would only infuriate her more. When the elevator doors slid closed behind her, I bit out a curse and sagged against the wall.

"What happened?" Sherrie asked.

"I told her we were looking into Rink and that we only needed the first witness to start a chain reaction that would blow up his career and take him out of commission for good. She said I was as good as calling her a coward for not speaking up and accused me of trying to blow up her life again."

Sherrie didn't say anything, just gave me a look full of concern and sympathy.

"What do I do? Go after her?"

"No. She told you not to. Respect that. And maybe I have the silver lining here." She handed me the folder she'd carried into my office. "I found someone willing to come forward. Heather Giles, an intern from seven years ago, and she thinks she has a friend who will speak up too. Apparently, they bonded over their time in Rink's office, and they've both gotten out of politics, so they're willing to speak out."

I took the folder. "Why these two? Why now?"

"Heather got married a couple of years ago and just had a daughter. Said it got her thinking about the world she's going to grow up in, and Heather wanted to do her part to make it better. Her friend, Madison, isn't a sure thing yet, but Heather thinks she may be able to talk her into coming forward too."

I tapped the folder against my palm. "It's unraveling."

She nodded. "Yeah, boss. I think it is. Finally."

I worked eighteen-hour days for the next week, first sitting in on the depositions of Heather Giles, then her friend, Madison, who decided to come forward too. Once I had their depositions, I went back to each of the previous victims who hadn't wanted to come forward. It meant back-to-back trips to New York and Philadelphia, but by the end of the week, we had five women ready to speak out against Rink.

The snake would not survive the scandal, not in the current political climate. And his governor would get a chance to appoint someone to serve out the rest of Rink's term, someone with the same political values but a true moral core. Someone who hadn't been corrupted by power.

I'd met Brooke too late to protect her from Rink. But at least I could make sure he never had a chance to prey on another bright-eyed idealist again.

I only wished I could tell Brooke, but she hadn't returned any of my texts over the last week, not even acknowledging my apologies.

I didn't know any other way to show her how sorry I was, but at least I could do this for her: Rink was done.

CHAPTER TWENTY-FOUR

Brooke

I drove home barely able to see the road through the red mist of my anger.

At Ian for sure.

But mostly at myself.

Of course Ian's interest hadn't been in me. Why would it be? He'd told me that he usually dated ambitious career women, not high school biology teachers who were content to live in the country with sawdust in their hair half the time.

All those leading questions he'd asked to try to get to know me better…those weren't genuine interest on his part. That was detective work. He was investigating Rink.

Rink deserved it. He deserved every bad thing coming to him if Ian was able to turn up any dirt.

My time in Rink's office had stripped away every illusion I'd ever had about powerful men. At least, the ones in politics. He'd lied to the public so convincingly for so long about who he was that I didn't believe the one warning I'd been given; when an aide I barely knew from a Midwest senator's office sought me out in the congressional cafeteria once to give me a vague warning about Rink, I'd brushed her off. Her boss was junior to Rink on the appropriations committee, and he'd benefit from a Rink scandal.

But she'd been right, and I'd been so wrong.

So painfully, terrifyingly wrong.

And wrong in a way that was almost impossible to prove.

What Rink had done to me in his office that night...I'd gotten away from him before he could push things as far as he'd wanted to. There was no physical evidence to take to the police beyond a torn skirt, a blouse with a missing button, and some pictures of me with some vague red marks. I was grateful for that, at least. I was grateful that he'd done no lasting physical harm.

But I'd still spent a year working with a therapist to get over the scarring no one could see, the raw places inside my mind where all my illusions, trust, and idealism had been ripped away.

Someday I'd be ready to trust another man, but maybe it would have to be someone like Noah Redmond, someone I started out with as truly just friends, something that would grow slowly over a long time, so I had a chance to study him, watch him in all kinds of settings to see how much integrity he really had.

Look what had happened when I had let my attraction to Ian hijack my personal judgment. My hormones and silly romanticism sent me to DC on the off-chance that I might see him. I'd talked myself into believing that he was the good man Miss Lily claimed he was. I'd wanted to believe that the electricity that sparked between us was something real.

"Ha." The laugh tore out of me, bitter and not at all funny.

Ian had swum with sharks and become one. Except that wasn't fair to sharks. He'd gone from thinking I was a gold digger to pretending to be into me so he could take down Rink. He wanted me to put my reputation, my job, *everything* on the line so he could score a victory for his firm.

No way.

I'd love to see Rink pay, and I had made him do it quite literally by threatening a lawsuit so big that he offered me a huge settlement to keep me quiet. I would have gone after him through the cops, but my mother had assessed it all with a lawyer's eye and confirmed that I didn't have enough for them to open an investigation that would stick. Without hard evidence, witnesses, corroborating statements... I'd had nothing. And even if I had those things, there was still no guarantee that Rink's connections wouldn't protect him. I'd be hung out to dry as an opportunist and a gold digger.

Either way, my career in DC was over, and I'd known it. So I took the money and walked, determined to build beauty from ashes. That was a phrase my favorite resident of Landsdowne used to say when she talked about turning failures into successes. I'd never really understood it until Rink forced me to burn my life down when I wouldn't let him take what he wanted just because he wanted it.

But no matter how often Ian bragged that he was good at his job, there was no way he would be able to find anything that would stick to Rink. And it was wrong to try to guilt me into offering myself up as leverage.

I drove the rest of the way home fifteen miles over the speed limit, and my anger could have pushed me higher if the roads were less winding.

I wasn't any less furious when I pulled into my driveway, and when I climbed up to my front door, I went out of my way to kick the box with the swing in it.

It took me forever to fall asleep that night, and I didn't wake up in a much better mood. My anger had cooled but my disappointment ran even deeper.

I spent Sunday ripping out old carpet upstairs, cutting and rolling it into rolls I could haul to the backyard by myself. I'd have to rent a truck to take it all to the dump, but the hard, heavy work helped burn off more of my mood. Ian texted a couple of times, but I ignored them. The first couple of lines I could see in each showed that he was at least trying to apologize instead of pressuring me into coming forward, but I wasn't in the mood for apologies. Or Ian.

When I rolled into school Monday morning, I felt almost normal. I got permission from the principal to turn a space in the school quad into a community garden. It was a 10 x 8 foot square of dirt surrounded by a low wall for students to sit. Ferns grew inside it but not well. The spot was too sunny for them, and it wasn't doing anything to beautify the campus. It was a perfect place to start a small garden, and I'd already looked into the supplies I'd need and come up with a game plan.

I stopped by Grace's store on the way home, smiling with grim satisfaction as the high total appeared in the register screen.

"This might be the kind of thing you could get the PTA to fundraise for," Grace said, noticing my look.

"It's okay. I set aside funds for this."

She eyed me for a minute as she typed up the invoice for delivery of the topsoil I'd ordered. "I know it's none of my business, but—"

"But that doesn't ever seem to stop people in Creekville from getting into mine anyway."

She grinned. "True that. But I have to say, you're going to go broke if you keep spending out of pocket like this for your classes."

I leaned forward and met her eye with another smile. "I really, really won't." I wasn't kidding about having made Rink pay. He'd paid me over a million dollars to keep my mouth shut.

Grace shook her head like she wasn't so sure, but she finished ringing me up without further comment.

I was halfway toward the door when I turned and went back to the register. "Have I thanked you a million billion times for helping me with all your advice and connections yet?"

"Yeah, but it's nice to have someone who actually takes my advice. A lot of the men who come in here don't believe me until they do a thing wrong their way, then they'll do it mine. But you can thank me again," she grinned. "I don't get tired of it."

I studied her for a second, really looking. She was probably about my age, her dark brown hair gathered in a ponytail, no makeup that I could see, but she was pretty in a quiet way. I'd only ever seen her in her work uniform, a shirt with the name of the hardware store and jeans. I didn't know much about her, but she always seemed to watch the world like she was secretly amused, whether she was helping me wrangle a rented floor sander up my stairs or gently explaining to someone's grandpa that he needed a different plumbing piece than the one he was asking for.

"Hey, Grace, would you want to get dinner some time? Miss Lily is my best friend in town right now, and I adore her, but she's kind of done for the day at 7:00 PM. Could be fun to have someone to grab a movie or dinner with."

She took a second to reply, and I rushed into the pause. "Sorry, is it weird that I asked? It probably is. I used to be good at socializing, but maybe I've forgotten how."

Grace shook her head and smiled. "No, it's not weird. I think I might be the one who's acting weird. I just..." She paused again. "I've kind of made a point of not getting too tangled up with people around here since I've been back the last couple of years. I don't plan to stay long term, and it seemed easier that way. But I think I'd love to grab dinner some time."

"Okay, cool. Thanks for not thinking I'm weird."

"Yeah, sure," she said. "Thanks for asking. The first part of your order should be in by Tuesday. The store closes at 6:00. What if you came by then to pick it up and then we'll grab something to eat?"

"Great. See you then." I waved and left, satisfied that both the garden and a new friendship was on their way to existence.

At home, Miss Lily was waiting for me in the garden like she'd known exactly when I would show up. She wore her gardening clogs and had her tote on the ground beside her. "Afternoon, Brooke. How was school?"

"Fine. I found a spot and got permission to put in the garden. Even started ordering supplies from Grace. I knew exactly what I needed thanks to your tutoring out here."

"Good. Tell me what you're going to plant."

I knelt to weed the squash and went through my plans with her, talking about all the lessons I would be able to teach about each point of the process. "I honestly don't know how anyone teaches biology without *having* a garden," I concluded.

"Hands on is always best. Makes it real for them while their brains are still trying to develop their abstract thinking skills. But enough about work. How goes life otherwise?"

Something about the way she asked it put me on guard. She was trying too hard to sound casual.

"It's good." I left it at that, waiting to see which way she would dig.

"Had a good visit with your parents?"

"Yes. They're busy as ever. My mom still thinks Creekville is a phase."

"You came home sooner than I expected. Didn't think I'd see your car until Sunday night."

I concentrated on pulling out an especially stubborn weed. It came loose but tried to take a bunch of soil with it. I smashed the clod and shook it back to its garden furrow, tossing aside the weed without remorse. "Let me guess; you talked to Ian."

"He did mention that he saw you this weekend, yes." She peered over the edge of her sunglasses. "I found it interesting that you didn't mention seeing him."

I didn't know what to say here. It wasn't like I was going to trash Ian to his own grandmother. "It was just in passing. Met up for lunch."

"And how did it go?"

"Fine. Good sandwiches."

"Brooke Spencer, that is not what I'm talking about, and you know it. Don't play clueless. It's unbecoming."

I sighed. "What did Ian say about it?"

"Not much. Mentioned that he'd seen you and asked if you were all right. Wouldn't tell me why he was asking. So. Are you all right?"

"Miss Lily, I adore you, and I know you'd love to see Ian and I get together, but it's not going to happen. We're not a good fit."

"Nonsense," she said, her voice calm as ever. "Eight decades buys you a lot of wisdom, and I haven't been wrong about a match in twenty years. If I say a couple doesn't have what it takes to make it, I'm right, and when I think two people are meant for each other, I'm also right. That's not bragging," she added, waving a gloved hand in my direction like she was preempting any argument. "It's fact. I have never once had an instinct about a couple and gotten it wrong either way."

"There's always a first time," I mumbled.

"Did you just sass me?" Her eyes narrowed. "Say it outright or don't say it at all."

"Fine," I said, pulling off my gloves and tossing them in my garden tote. "I admit this is the first time I've ever known you to be wrong about anything, but you are dead wrong about me and Ian. There's not a worse mismatch that I can think of. I think you missed having him come around so much that you talked yourself into believing that he and I were a good fit."

I scrambled to my feet, not daring to look at her in case I'd offended her. But she was quiet for so long that I finally snuck a glance. Instead of a frown, she was grinning as she went back to pulling weeds like nothing had happened.

"Miss Lily?"

"Yes, honey?"

"You're not mad?"

"Of course not. Why would I be mad when you're so clearly in love with my grandson?"

I gasped. "I am not!"

"You are. Or very close to it. Otherwise, he wouldn't make you so mad."

This delusion was worse than her being angry. I hated the idea of dooming her to disappointment. I didn't want to go around destroying any of her illusions about Ian, but I didn't want her clinging to the vain hope that he and I would end up together, either. It seemed a poor way to repay all her kindness.

"We won't work, Miss Lily. Our val—priorities are too different." I caught myself before accusing him of having poor values. "Night and day different. City and country different. If it makes you feel better, I admit he's as handsome as you said he was, and he's definitely charming, but we don't have enough in common to work."

She narrowed her eyes at me. "Charming is a word for men who are all flash and no substance, and that's not Ian. Why don't you tell me what really happened this weekend? And don't tiptoe around me. How many times do I have to remind you I'm eighty? I don't break easily, so you can stop treating me like I'm fragile. Just spit it out, girl. Can't fix it if I don't know what's broke."

"There's nothing to fix." I hesitated, still unsure if I wanted to lay out the whole story, but there wasn't one thing Miss Lily hadn't worn me down about that she wanted me to do yet.

"Are you realizing it's easier to tell me now since I'll get it out of you eventually?" she asked, her eyes twinkling.

"Yes, ma'am."

"Smart woman. Now spill."

"Well, you know Ian and I had a rough start," I began.

"A rare miscalculation on my part," she acknowledged.

"The thing is, I thought we'd gotten past that. But I told him I didn't think us dating made much sense because his career is in DC, and I'm never going back. I didn't see the point. Still, I just…"

"Found yourself thinking about my rogue of a grandson anyway?"

That wrung a smile from me. "Something like that. I was worried that spending all that time in cutthroat DC politics had maybe…" I didn't want to say "corrupted" him and offend Miss Lily. "Had maybe jaded him too much."

"Too much for what?"

"Me, basically. He spends all his time in an environment that I had to leave or be consumed by. But then we'd hang out, and it was so simple and easy. And I thought I was wrong. I kept waiting for him to come back so I could explore it more and see."

"You waited for him to come back after you told him to stay away?"

"He told you about that?"

"Of course. To be fair, he was trying to make sure I left you alone and didn't meddle."

"It wasn't that I told him to go away, exactly." I toed the dirt, remembering the conversation on my porch. "It was more that I told him to talk to me from his side of the creek and kicked the bridge down between us."

KISS ME NOW

"I do love a good metaphor," she said. "But you changed your mind?"

"At first. I went out to DC to meet him on his turf since he'd kept coming to mine." I hesitated, searching for the most diplomatic way to say the next part. "I know you love Ian, and I'm not trying to badmouth him, but the thing is, it turns out he was more interested in me as a witness to a case he's working on than anything else."

Miss Lily's gaze sharpened. "That doesn't sound like Ian at all."

I shrugged. I couldn't tell her anything else without it sounding like a character assassination.

"Keep going," she said. "I'm not going to get mad at you for reporting facts as you see them. I know you're fair-minded. But it would save me the trouble of digging the details out of Ian. Come on to the house for some sweet tea, and we'll talk it through."

It was the last thing I wanted to do, but there was no way I'd hurt Miss Lily's feelings. I'd give back my million-plus dollars first.

We settled into her breakfast nook with a cold glass of iced tea in front of each of us, the A/C cooling us down.

"Go ahead," Miss Lily prompted.

So I told her about Senator Rink harassing me, getting the settlement when I realized I couldn't win a prosecution, starting over out here away from the disillusionment of DC politics. How Ian and I had connected, and I pushed him away, then found I couldn't stay away myself so I made up a flimsy excuse to see him in DC. How wandering the zoo with him had been perfect and easy, and everything had been going great until he asked me to make a public statement about Rink.

She took it all in without interrupting, only sipped and listened. When I was done, she sat in quiet for a moment. "Just to clarify," she said. "You say he didn't bring up speaking out about Rink until his assistant burst in and blurted out his name?"

"Correct."

"Do you think they coordinated that, or do you think she genuinely didn't realize you were there?"

I thought back. Sherrie had looked honestly startled to realize Ian had someone in his office. "I think she was surprised."

"So it's possible he brought it up only because she'd already mentioned Rink." She set her glass down and patted at her mouth with her linen napkin. "I think you read him wrong. If Ian had wanted to drag you into this, he would have done it before you showed up in DC. He'd have been out here trying to talk you into it. And I don't think for a second that he'd try to fool you with seduction or anything like that."

I blinked to clear the image of Ian's granny talking about seduction.

"He's too straightforward for that. But either way, he still didn't come out here. It only came up because his assistant inadvertently brought it up without any idea you were there. So it sounds like he's been working on this for a while without contacting you about it once, correct?"

"Correct," I said, still not convinced.

"Knowing Ian, my guess is that he felt like it would be unethical *not* to broach it with you, and he'd been avoiding you and trying to solve the problem from a different angle. But once you were right there, he probably felt he didn't have a choice but to ask."

It had to be impossible for Miss Lily to hear a critique of Ian and not want to defend him. I wasn't going to try to change her mind, but I knew what I knew about how it had felt to sit in his office and have him ask me to confront the monster who'd tried to ruin my life.

I changed course, not willing to cause a strain between us. "Ian and I aren't a good fit and trying to think about a love life right now stresses me out. I think I'd rather worry about solvable problems. Can we talk about how I'm going to keep the students out of the garden when it goes in?"

She gave me a long look. "One last thing before we move on. I dislike DC as much as you do, but I have never made the mistake of believing true public servants are bad people. I wouldn't mind if Ian stayed there if he'd switch to a career more focused on doing good than digging up bad, because as much as I know someone has to do the dirty work, I think it can wear people down, and I worry about him." She leaned over and patted my hand. "I'll let it go now. Let's talk about keeping hooligans out of your turnips. I have a few ideas."

We went back to work in the garden for another hour, but I doubted I was good company for the rest of it. Despite a desire to forget Ian altogether, Miss Lily's words kept running through my mind. *He probably didn't feel he had a choice but to ask.*

Maybe what I was maddest about was the fact that it had pulled up everything that had happened with Rink when all I wanted to do was push it away. But that had been happening before I even stepped foot in Ian's office. Being in DC was enough by itself to constantly remind me of why I left it—who forced me to leave it.

Maybe what I was maddest about was that Rink was still standing, and that wasn't how it was supposed to be. The good guys are supposed to win.

The thought preyed on me more and more over the next two weeks, popping up during quiet moments between classes, or during the mindless prep work I was doing to get the upstairs rooms ready for painting. Normally, that was my time to think about lesson planning, but more and more often, my conscience kept nudging me. *What if Ian didn't have enough without my testimony to take down Rink?* Did it make me complicit in keeping Rink in power?

By Thursday, I could only conclude after a sleepless night that if a statement from me was enough to establish a pattern for the senator's behavior, I needed to make it.

But that meant violating my non-disclosure agreement, and Rink could sue me to get back every penny of the settlement. I'd spent over $300,000 between buying out my cousins and investing in renovation upgrades. The rest of it was sitting in an investment account that I could cash out and return, and I'd have to take out a mortgage on the house to repay that part of the settlement. I didn't know if I'd even be approved for one on a starting teacher's salary. But I'd spent most of the night staring at the ceiling, trying to do the math, only to come up with the same answer: I probably *wouldn't* be able to pay back what I'd spent from the settlement. But I couldn't live with myself if I didn't come forward.

Possible bankruptcy was worth the risk if it meant getting Rink's moral bankruptcy out of office. If it meant he couldn't hurt another woman ever again.

I waited until my lunch break at school to send Ian the text I couldn't take back. *Wouldn't* take back.

I'll come forward on Rink.

His reply was immediate. *No need. We got him.*

I stared at my phone, stunned. "We got him," I repeated out loud. What did that mean? I did a search of social media and news sites, but there wasn't any mention of Rink in the headlines, and a scandal with him would definitely mean headlines.

I texted back. *Not seeing anything in the news...*

Will break next week, Ian responded. *Will tell you all about it.*

When? I asked.

Soon. But first, I AM SORRY. Wish I knew how to fix things with you.

Noah was supposed to be coming by for lunch as usual, but I texted him that I had to take a raincheck. Instead, I sat by myself at my desk and re-read Ian's message a dozen times.

It sounded like he meant fixing things between *us*, but there wasn't really an us. I hadn't let that get off the ground.

I regretted that. I shouldn't have pushed him away.

We made no sense together in a lot of ways. I wasn't leaving Creekville. He wasn't leaving DC. If we dated long-distance and it worked out, at some point one of us was going to have to close the two-hour gap, and that meant one of us giving up a career for the other.

I wouldn't do that for him. But I also wouldn't ask him to do that for me.

So what was the point of regretting that we hadn't worked out?

There was no point.

But when I pulled into my empty driveway in front of my quiet house, the regret almost consumed me.

I had broken a relationship that could never work.

But it didn't keep me from wanting Ian anyway.

CHAPTER TWENTY-FIVE

Ian

I hit the road Friday morning. It was after rush hour which meant the rare chance to speed on the beltway on the way out of town.

I could feel the weight of the city and its problems slip from my shoulders as it retreated in the rearview mirror. It had been a hard two weeks, hopping on and off planes and trains to interview suspects. Heather, the former intern, had been the key, like I'd hoped. And yesterday I had taken a statement from a sixth victim. They were each ready to speak their truth about Rink, whatever the consequences.

The only reason I needed to bring it up to Brooke was to apologize for trying to pressure her into stepping forward too. We wouldn't need her to, and I was sorry I'd tried. After listening to each of these women, I couldn't blame her for trying to close the door on that period of her life forever. Rink was indeed a monster, a manipulative and devious snake who had abused his authority for twenty years.

No more. The story would be all over the news by next week, and Rink would be forced to resign. Even more importantly, his reputation would precede him. There was little shot of getting a criminal conviction against him, but at least women entering his orbit in the future would know what kind of man they were dealing with.

I turned my attention to the road ahead. It led to Brooke. And until yesterday, I wouldn't have taken it.

I'd tried so hard to respect her boundaries. I'd planned to give her all the distance she wanted, maybe not even see Gran again until Thanksgiving. It was more than that though. I'd learned a few things about Brooke in the few weeks I'd known her, but a thing I knew for certain was that she dove headlong into things she believed in. The way she'd thrown herself into learning to garden. How she immersed herself in prepping to teach high school kids. It'd made it harder to accept her decision to stay quiet about Rink. She hadn't struck me as the type who could be silenced by anything or anyone if her cause was just.

Then I'd learned over the last two weeks just what a scumbag Rink was. I couldn't imagine being at his mercy, becoming his victim and feeling like I had no voice to demand restitution or change. But I'd kept butting up against this feeling that if anyone could do it, it would be Brooke.

Only she hadn't.

I'd held it against her, even though I didn't want to. Even though I told myself all the logical reasons why it was wrong to hold her to that standard. Even though we had enough evidence now without her to nail Rink completely.

I'd lost my illusions about people and pedestals a long time ago. Probably by year two as the firm's investigator. But it turned out I'd put Brooke on one anyway, and I couldn't forgive her for being as human as the rest of us.

I'd wanted her to be a superhero and she'd committed the sin of being mortal.

It was so stupid to blame her for me being disillusioned again. But she'd been something fresh and bright in the stagnant DC swamp, and it had hurt when she was just as human as the rest of us.

And then she texted.

Like a freaking superhero.

A superhero who was ready to risk Rink's retribution, public shaming, a revival of the rumors.

But she'd texted and said she would do it. She would upset the carefully constructed life she'd built for herself over the last two years to come forward and speak out against Rink despite the extremely high cost to herself.

That wasn't the kind of woman you let go.

At least, it wasn't the kind of woman I could let go. Even if all she had to offer me was friendship, I'd take it. People as real and as good as Brooke, people without ulterior motives, who shot straight and showed up as themselves in every setting ... that was rare. And I wasn't going to treat a chance at friendship with her as a second place finish.

I'd be lying if I didn't admit that buried somewhere deep down, there was a hope for something more. But I'd take whatever she was able to give. No matter what, if I wanted to get us back on the right footing, I owed her a big apology. The unmistakable kind. The kind that spoke through actions, not just words.

The kind of actions that said *I love you*, even if she wasn't ever ready to hear me say those words.

But if she ever *was* ready, then I would be too.

Somewhere between her mushroom hunting and the panda exhibit, I'd begun falling for her, but when she'd texted that she wanted to speak out, I'd tumbled completely.

If I thought she genuinely had no feelings for me, I'd stay in DC until I couldn't avoid coming to see Gran. But a woman who didn't have feelings for me wouldn't have kissed me like that in the woods. She wouldn't have made an excuse to come see me in the city. And it wouldn't have hurt her when I asked her to be a witness.

She had feelings for me. I knew it.

But I needed to prove to her that I was worthy of her trust. That I could be the kind of man that she deserved.

I pushed the accelerator and watched the speedometer climb. I had a plan, and I couldn't wait to put it into action.

CHAPTER TWENTY-SIX

Brooke

When the final bell rang on Friday, I followed the last kid right out of the door. Normally, I worked for another hour or two in my classroom, getting everything ready for Monday, catching up on grading. There never seemed to be enough time to get it all done.

But today, I just wanted to go home. I wanted to go home, crawl into bed, dive into a beach book full of beautiful people and solvable problems, and I wanted to forget all of mine. I wanted to read a story about people who figured out how to get love right, because I had failed at it so badly.

I hoped against all reason that if Ian did make it to his gran's this weekend that he would come over to declare his undying love and sweep me off my feet.

But why would he? I had practically taken out a billboard shouting: I DON'T WANT TO DATE YOU.

Only…it didn't seem to matter how many times I explained to myself that it didn't make sense, or that my biology degree told me my brain had all the control of my body: my heart was NOT having it. My heart wanted Ian. His jokes. His cheerful help in my house. His kindness to his grandmother. His sharp mind. His teasing.

His kisses.

Oh, those kisses.

I'd found myself reliving those kisses in the woods multiple times a day. It didn't matter if I was grading pop quizzes, pulling weeds, or wrestling carpet. That kiss would flash in my head, and suddenly I'd find my cheeks flushed—and if I let myself follow the memory—my palms sweaty.

I drove home, the route almost automatic now, my mind on what I would say or do if Ian came to Miss Lily's this weekend.

We still had some big obstacles in the way of a relationship. I didn't want to move to DC. There wasn't much scope for a private investigator in sleepy Creekville. And maybe it was stupid to worry about those things when we might not work out. We may not ever have to worry about a discussion of how we fit into each other's lives.

But the way I felt about Ian...I'd never felt like this before. I'd had a semi-serious boyfriend in college, but he'd never made me feel like even the air I breathed crackled with energy the way Ian did when he was around. I didn't need Miss Lily's wisdom to tell me that was rare. She'd known all along that Ian and I were a match, thus her ridiculous scheme to lure him home to meet me.

Maybe Ian was only coming back this weekend to say he was sorry. But if he knew that I had changed my mind, that I wanted to figure out where this thing went...

The rest was details. I could get a teaching job in DC. The schools there probably needed me more than Lincoln did.

I tightened my hands on the steering wheel. All I knew for sure was that finding out how real these feelings between Ian and I were was worth it. I stepped on the gas and leaned forward, like that would somehow make my car go even faster. I was anxious to get home and get ready for Ian. I'd choose a pretty dress, a bottle of wine, and practice my best apology for pushing him away so many times.

Because this feeling? It felt a lot like love, and that was worth saving.

I was straining to look for Ian's car in Miss Lily's driveway before I even turned into my own, and when the sun glinted off the sleek dark blue of his BMW, my grip relaxed on the steering wheel even as butterflies exploded in my stomach.

Ian had come. At least I had a chance to make this right.

I turned into my own driveway, but it wasn't until I stepped out of my car that I realized my front porch had undergone a renovation: the porch swing was now hanging from the perfect spot on the side of the porch.

And Ian was sitting in the middle of it.

My heart gave the stutter skip it'd gotten the last few times I'd seen him. More biology I didn't understand.

"Ian?"

He rose from the swing and came to the top of the stairs to meet me as I made my way up. "Hey," he said, taking the tote from my shoulder. "I hope it's okay that I put it up. Seemed like the perfect spot."

"It is," I said glancing toward it. He'd even stolen some pillows I recognized from Miss Lily's family room to brighten it up. "It looks really good there. But…"

"Wait," he said. "I'm sorry to interrupt, but I've kind of got a speech, if that's okay?"

He looked at me with more uncertainty than I'd ever seen on his face, and I gave a nod. I wasn't sure I'd found the right words myself yet anyway.

"I've always been raised to respect women and to listen when they tell you what they want. And I heard you loud and clear when you said you only wanted to be friends. But I also think you're the kind of woman who appreciates having all the facts before making a decision. So I wondered if I could give you some additional data. For science?"

A small smile tugged at my lips. "Okay. For science."

"I have this plan to be in this swing every Friday afternoon when you get home. And to sit in it with you every Monday evening before I drive back to the city Tuesday morning. Because a lot of the work I do can be done remotely, and my bosses signed off on it. I'll be in the office Tuesday through Friday morning, and be back here to greet you after work every Friday afternoon. Sometimes I'll have to stay in the city over the weekend, but Sherrie can handle most of what comes up without me."

"But—"

"There's more. I'm not saying it has to be that way. It's only if you want to. I'll respect you and take it as your final word if you don't, but..." He ran his hand through his hair, pushing the strands askew, and I wanted to reach up and brush the pieces back into place. "But I keep thinking about how every minute I've spent with you, even when we're arguing or just eating sandwiches, makes me feel more alive than anything I've done in the city has in years. And I'm hoping...I'm hoping it's not my imagination. That you feel it too?"

He was a supremely confident guy, so much so that I'd cussed him as cocky a few times, but there was only vulnerability in his eyes now.

I reached over and took his free hand, sliding mine into his so he wouldn't have another second of doubt. "The idea of seeing you on my porch swing every Friday makes it a little hard to breathe, but I think it's in a good way?"

He gave a small laugh. "I don't know how I'm supposed to take that."

"Maybe we need more science investigation. What does it mean when the idea of seeing you—no, that actually seeing you right here in this moment—makes my heart race, my mouth go dry, my palms sweat, and my stomach flip?"

He pretended to think about it. "It could mean that you're having a panic attack. But there's a pretty good test. Do you also have weak knees?"

"Not yet."

"Then for science, I think you probably need to kiss me now."

"For science," I agreed as he pulled me toward him. When he kissed me, the whole world became the soft rasp of his breath and the sound of my own heartbeat. His lips were gentle at first, but as I leaned into him the kiss deepened. He pulled me tight against him, and I had a whole new host of symptoms to report. Wild, delicious, shivery symptoms.

He pulled back. "How are your knees?" he asked softly.

"Weak. Very weak. And my heart is pounding too."

"So what does the science tell us?"

"More experiments needed."

His eyebrow went up and his eyes danced. "I might know more about the science here than you do."

"Tell me," I said, running a finger across his bottom lip.

"It means you might be in danger of falling for me as hard as I've fallen for you."

I stopped tracing his lip to meet his eyes. "You have?"

"Deeply. It's kind of a problem."

My stomach flipped again. "Not if I've fallen for you too."

He rested his forehead against mine. "You have?"

"Deeply." I rested my hands against his chest and reveled in how solid and warm he felt against my palms which itched with a new symptom: a need to explore him more.

He took a deep breath. "Just so we're clear, I'm saying I love you, Brooke Spencer."

"And just so I'm clear, Ian Greene, I'm saying I love you back. So what do we do now?" I asked.

"Kiss her again!" Miss Lily shouted, and we looked over to find her and Mary, standing on my side of the garden, holding on to each other and grinning like fools.

"When she's right, she's right," Ian said. And then he kissed me again, and I discovered a new symptom: Ian's kisses made me forget about everything but him.

EPILOGUE

Grace Winters stepped back to stare up at the bower she'd built. It was sturdy, but more importantly, it would be high enough for the groom who'd be standing under it tomorrow. Ian Greene was a tall man, but he'd have plenty of clearance.

She gave the frame another hard shake, but it held steady. Good. She'd done good work.

When she retreated down the grassy aisle flanked on either side by white chairs and studied it again from a distance, she was even more satisfied. Lily Greene had worked with the florist in town to use as many flowers from her own grounds as possible to fill in the arbor her grandson would be wed beneath.

"It's gorgeous," Grace said out loud.

"Agreed," said a voice behind her. "And I love it. Thank you for building it for me. You didn't have to do that."

Grace spun, not realizing Brooke had joined her. "What are you doing out here? Shouldn't you be getting ready for the rehearsal dinner?"

Brooke smiled and slipped her hands into the pockets of her pink joggers. "It'll take me ten minutes to get ready. I wanted to come out here while it was quiet. I'm afraid I won't notice the details once the wedding starts. You look great, by the way."

Grace glanced down at her dress, a light and pretty confection of gauzy blue fabric that draped gently from spaghetti straps to skim just above her knees. "Thanks for letting me borrow it. I feel almost bad for feeling so pretty in it. I don't want to outshine the bride."

Brooke laughed and came to stand beside her and study the arbor. "You're welcome. But I think we're both going to be outshone by Gran's flowers."

"She did a great job, but you're already gorgeous. And your gown is to die for. Ian won't even realize he's standing beneath a thousand flowers when he's looking at you."

Brooke slipped an arm around Grace's waist and gave her a side hug. "I'm so glad we're friends. It's been a wild year. You've kept me sane. And, you know, made my house livable."

"Is your mom still nervous about the short engagement?"

Brooke shrugged, not a single doubt on her face. "I don't know. It doesn't matter. I've known Ian almost a year, but it didn't even take me a month to realize he's the one for me. She's had five months to get used to the idea of engagement. I think she's more annoyed that we aren't doing the wedding in McLean so she can invite all her country club friends."

"Sometimes it sounds like a completely different world when you talk about life before you came to Creekville," Grace said. "And it's almost like our lives are inverses of each other. You running away to a small town, me wanting to get out of it."

"Well, for selfish reasons, I'm glad you've been here. It's been kind of a long time since I've had a best friend. But if you ever decide you're really done here, I'll help you pack to leave."

Grace threw her arm around Brooke to give her a full hug. "I know you would. That's why I love you."

They'd been friendly enough when Brooke first came to town, even gone out for girls' night a couple of times, but it wasn't until Brooke roped her into helping her remodel an upstairs bathroom that they'd really become friends. In fact, when Brooke had tried to pay her, Grace wouldn't accept it, so Brooke had overpaid for all her materials to keep it even. They'd spent four weeks in a row working on the remodel on weeknights when Ian was in DC, laughing and drinking more coffee than any human should in a single day.

Grace had loved having a front row seat to watching Brooke's relationship with Ian unfold. These two were couple goals.

Well, they were the goal if she intended to stay in Creekville, which she didn't. Not forever. But for as long as her mom needed her, she'd be here. She just wouldn't make the mistake of forming the kind of attachments with anyone else that might keep her here.

"Brooke?" It was Ian's voice, and it sounded like he was calling from the direction of Miss Lily's back patio.

Grace smiled as Brooke's face lit up. "You two just do not get sick of each other, do you?"

"Nope," Brooke agreed. "And I want to soak in every single minute because I'm going to be a work widow soon. For five months. Quantico."

Grace's eyes widened. "FBI training?"

Brooke nodded, grinning. "Ian found out yesterday that he was accepted."

"That's amazing! I'll try not to think about what that means for you leaving me."

"You aren't planning to stay anyway," Brooke reminded her.

"True enough."

Ian called for Brooke again. "Brooke Spencer soon-to-be Greene?"

Brooke turned toward his voice and smiled. "Sounds like it's time to get this rehearsal going. You ready?"

"Yeah, I'll be right behind you."

Brooke nodded and hurried off toward the sound of Ian's voice, calling back that she was coming.

And Grace stood in the bridal garden by herself for one last moment, once again admiring the arbor, without the faintest clue that everything in her own life was about to change.

ACKNOWLEDGMENTS

I really don't know how I ever wrote books before I found my writing group. Teri Bailey Black, Aubrey Hartman, Brittany Larsen, Tiffany Odekirk, and Jen White make all my books better. Daily writing sprints over Zoom with Clarissa Kae and Esther Hatch have kept me going on days I didn't feel like working. And Jenny Proctor's constant cheerleading and super fast beta read convinced me that this was a book worth sharing with everyone. I owe thanks for this and several books to Cindy Ray and Camille Maynard for their proofreading and editing skills. I'm thankful to Emily Poole for her gardening consultations. Mistakes are definitely all my own. It's been a lifetime since I spent time in my father's garden. Many thanks to Bryan Eisenbise for helping me plot a fictional crime. Thank you to Shawn Larsen for the law bits that I ended up not using. And thank you to anyone who answered questions about Virginia government, Washington traffic, home renovations, or the million other little questions I had as I worked through this story. Thank you to Raneé for her patience and formatting skills. Last but certainly not least, much love and gratitude to Kenny and my kids for their constant encouragement and support.

ABOUT THE AUTHOR

Melanie Bennett Jacobson is an avid reader, amateur cook, and champion shopper. She grew up in Louisiana but now lives in Southern California with her husband, children, and a naughty miniature schnauzer. She subs high school English for fun when she's not writing. Melanie holds an MFA in Writing from the Vermont College of Fine Arts. To find other books by Melanie Jacobson or to get a free book from her, no newsletter signup required, please visit her website at www.melaniejacobson.net.

Printed in Great Britain
by Amazon